MEDIAPOLIS PUBLIC LIBRARY
128 N. ORCHARD ST.
MEDIAPOLIS, IA 52637

PRIME ASSET

8/19

Help us Rate this book…
Put your initials on the
left side and your rating
on the right side.
1 = Didn't care for
2 = It was O.K.
3 = It was great

DATE DUE

AUG 2 3 2019 MRH		
NOV 2 1 2019		
DEC 1 0 2019		
MAR 2 3 2020		
MAR 2 8 2020		

MRH   1 2 ③
         1 2 ③
_____ 1 2 3
_____ 1 2 3
_____ 1 2 3
_____ 1 2
_____ 1 2
_____ 1 2
_____ 1 2
_____ 1 2 3
_____ 1 2 3
_____ 1 2 3
_____ 1 2 3
_____ 1 2 3
_____ 1 2 3

D1113137

PRINTED IN U.S.A.

PRIME

ASSET

A Corp Justice Novel
Book 3 of the Corps Justice Series

C. G. COOPER

ISBN: 1537755137
ISBN 13: 9781537755137

**Get any *Corps Justice* novel for free just for subscribing at
>> CG-COOPER.com <<**

To my amazing wife who never tires of proofing my writing, I love you, K, and couldn't do it without you!

To my entire family and amazing group of friends that have supported me unconditionally, you guys are awesome.

To our troops, active and retired, thank you for your service. God Bless.

EPISODE 1

CHAPTER 1

The shivering was gone. Adrenaline coursed through his body, fueling survival. The huge grizzly bear took another swipe as the young man retaliated with a short swing with his torch. Sparks flew as the errant swing grazed the side of the small alcove.

The bear didn't flinch. Instead, it pushed its head into the opening and unleashed a deafening roar. The grizzly's hot breath assaulted the trapped man as he tried to make himself as small as possible against the back of the hole. There was nowhere to go. He'd lost all his weapons except for the burning torch that was now almost out. What he wouldn't give for even a small knife. The only thing saving him from instant death was the fact that the bear couldn't fit through the alcove's entrance. But its claws could, and they'd already torn a jagged cut into the man's winter parka. It wouldn't be long until the bear figured out how to get more.

The man had no idea how the animal had followed him onto the narrow ledge. He'd underestimated the bear's tenacity and hunger. The park ranger had warned about the bears being hungrier than usual this year. Something about a shortage of berries. Shaking the thought from his head, the man reviewed his options. There were none. The best he could do was to wait and see if his attacker would leave. But that was unlikely given his current position.

The early fall blizzard continued to blow in as the bear tried to widen the opening. Suddenly, and without warning, the bear pulled its head out and turned around.

What's he doing? thought the man.

He chanced a peek out of the man-sized hole and watched the bear as it sniffed the air, almost looking like a dog as it searched.

The young man wouldn't have another chance. Squeezing out of the hole, the loud wind mercifully masking any sound, he stood not three feet from the distracted grizzly. He'd never make it if he took the path. The bear would win. Making up his mind, Cal Stokes sprinted the four feet to the ravine's ledge and jumped.

CHAPTER 2

TETON VILLAGE
JACKSON HOLE, WYOMING
TWO DAYS EARLIER, 4:24PM, SEPTEMBER 26TH

Days earlier, Cal Stokes and Daniel Briggs landed in the small Jackson Hole airport. If asked, they were in the area for a two week hunting trip.

Cal was in his early thirties, good-looking and just under six feet tall. He was dressed in jeans, boots and a distressed t-shirt. His brown hair was covered in a trucker's ball cap. After getting his bearings, he left his companion and proceeded to the Enterprise counter.

Briggs, a couple inches taller and a former Marine sniper, stayed behind and waited for their luggage. He shook out his shoulder length blonde hair and tied it back in a ponytail. Out of habit, he glanced around casually while bending down to retie his hiking boots. No obvious surveillance other than the airport security cameras. Five minutes later, Briggs hauled their four bags and two weapons cases out the sliding doors.

The temperature was still in the upper sixties as Briggs took a deep breath. He loved the outdoors. He'd never been to Wyoming. Now was his chance. As the newest employee of Stokes Security International, Daniel was also his employer's unofficial bodyguard. On SSI's official ledger he was listed as 'Security Contractor 3982.' The company did a lot of personal protection and surveillance overseas and had a legion of former military contractors around the globe. To any prying eyes, Daniel was one of them. To the majority owner of SSI, Calvin Stokes, Jr., he was a trusted advisor and friend.

Cal pulled up in a black Ford Excursion. After loading all their gear into the back, the two Marines got in. Briggs keyed the hotel's address into their GPS as Cal made a phone call.

"Trav, we're on our way to Teton Village." Travis Haden was CEO of SSI, a former Navy SEAL and Cal's cousin.

"Good. Trent, Dunn and Gaucho's boys are spread out on the next couple flights. They should all be there by noon tomorrow."

"Thanks again for setting that up. Any updates on Neil?" Neil Patel, one of Cal's best friends and SSI's head of Research and Development, had disappeared two days earlier. He'd been in Jackson Hole for a small conference with some of the world's top technology firms. It was an annual invite-only-event and Patel's third year attending. Haden had received a call from a friend attending the conference. The guy told Travis that Neil hadn't shown up for his lecture; something about the importance of battlefield innovation on civilian product development. The man was frantic because the entire group of enrollees was waiting anxiously for Patel's popular talk.

It wasn't like Neil to miss anything. After calling Patel's cell and hotel room repeatedly, they couldn't track him down. Finally, Travis placed a call to the hotel security staff and convinced them to search Neil's room. The head of security conducted the search personally. Neil's room was empty. Despite an unmade bed and used hotel toiletries in the bathroom, all of Patel's personal belongings were gone.

Due to the sensitive information Neil stored in his genius-level brain, Travis initiated a complete lockdown of SSI's systems. In spite of Patel's insistence to the contrary, Todd Dunn, SSI's head of internal security, had warned against allowing one of SSI's key assets to travel alone. Always planning for the worst, Dunn came up with a backstop: Neil was required to have a micro transmitter (of Neil's own design) surgically implanted in his ankle. It would lie dormant until needed. The transmitter allowed SSI to turn on the tracking feature and find Patel anywhere in the world.

The first thing Dunn did after getting the news from his boss was to turn on the tracking device. Nothing happened. That meant one of three things. One, the device malfunctioned. Two, Neil disabled the device. Three, someone had kidnapped Neil, extracted the transmitter, and destroyed it.

They had to plan for the worst. First, it wasn't natural for one of Neil's gadgets not to work. He'd tested it on multiple subjects, and it had always performed above expectations. Second, Neil had no reason to take the thing out. Third, Patel was a big target. If someone wanted to find a goldmine of technological knowledge, Neil was a human treasure trove. With his near photographic memory and world-class hacking skills (he regularly trolled the vaunted systems of organizations like the CIA, MI6 and FBI just for fun), he was an invaluable asset.

On the surface, things remained calm. Travis thanked the hotel security team and apologized for the inconvenience and had given them the excuse that he'd just found out that Neil left early due to a death in the family. He gave the same story to the colleague who'd called to ask about Patel.

Behind the scenes, SSI worked overtime. Not only was Patel a vital part of ongoing SSI operations and R&D, but, like a seasoned CIA station chief, Neil knew everything. His capture and the exposure of SSI's covert operations would mean disaster not just for the company, but for various players within the American government. There were implications all the way up to the President. It wasn't a scenario Travis wanted to have play out.

"Did you have Neil's guys go over the list of people attending the conference?" Cal asked.

"For the third time, yes, cuz. We're doing everything we can on this end. We haven't even had a whiff from any of our sources."

Cal huffed in frustration. He knew the headquarters team was doing everything they could, but Cal wasn't a patient man. Travis had even placed a secure call to the President to give him a heads-up. Because of Cal's recent rescue of the American President, the politician promised to help however he could.

"Sorry. I'm just worried."

"You and me both. I've been wracking my brain trying to figure this thing out. Have any wild ideas on your flight out?" asked Travis.

"I had too many ideas. Name one group of bad guys that wouldn't want their hands on Neil. It's like having the ultimate cyberweapon."

The two men were silent for a moment as they both tried to envision the possible fallout. It wouldn't be good. They had to get Neil back.

Cal switched gears. "How many people knew Neil was coming out for this conference?"

"Obviously everyone attending. That's just under fifty people. Then, of course, there's his staff here and our leadership team. Seventy-five people tops?"

Seventy-five people. It could be worse. "I assume you've already got our people doing background checks on all of them, right?"

"Yeah. Nothing yet. There are some competitors we need to take a closer look at, but I think the guy that organizes the conference has already done a pretty good job vetting attendees."

Cal figured that was the case. These were high-profile executives. Most of them probably had the equivalent of Top Secret clearances in the tech world. Still, at this point, everyone was a suspect.

"I've got a really bad feeling about this, Trav. Please let me know if you find out anything new. Me and the boys will hit the pavement here."

"No problem. Let's stay in touch."

Cal ended the call and put his phone in the cup holder. He'd hoped to have something to go on before starting the search. Best case, they'd find Neil soon. Worst case, someone had already shipped him off to another country.

Neil sat shivering in his small cell. He was wrapped in an old olive drab wool blanket. It wasn't much, but it warded off some of the chill.

The only light in the room came from a tiny window the size of a brick. He'd already tried banging on it but the damn thing felt like it was a foot thick. One of the guards paid him a visit after checking the window and gifted him with a hard jab in the sternum. The spot still hurt.

He laughed at the pettiness of the recollection. Compared to the rest of his predicament, the blow was a minor inconvenience. Neil had a bad feeling about why they'd kidnapped him as he'd walked back from the sushi restaurant two nights ago. It made it even worse that they'd known exactly where his remote locator was. That was, until they'd taken care of it.

Neil reached down to the neatly bandaged stump that used be his ankle and winced. At least they'd had the courtesy to knock him out and supposedly had a real doctor cut his foot off. *Look on the bright side, right?*

He sat back and adjusted his Prada eyeglasses. Neil wouldn't be walking out anytime soon, but he started to prepare mentally for whatever horrors awaited him. A small part of his subconscious hoped Cal would come bursting through the door at that very second.

"You're sure?" Nick Ponder asked into the phone.

"Yeah. They just landed. You want us to follow them?"

"No. I've got another team waiting in Teton Village. We already know they're staying at Hotel Terra. With the slow season it'll be easy to keep tabs on them. I want you to stick around and let me know when the rest of their guys land."

"Okay, boss."

Nick Ponder, a fifty-five year old former Green Beret, hung up the phone. He stood up from his simple metal desk and stretched his hulking six foot six frame. Over the past few years he'd grown out his beard into an unruly black tangle. He kept his head shaved bald. Being imposing and ruthless were two of Ponder's gifts. He'd learned it in the military and carried on the tradition when they'd kicked him out in 1996, and he'd started his own company.

He still worked out daily and could best most men half his age. Seven years ago he'd relocated his company headquarters to Wyoming. Ponder enjoyed the wilderness but liked the secluded fortress much more. There wasn't much he couldn't do out here. It was perfect for staying under the radar.

After the little incident with that prick Calvin Stokes Sr. back in 1999, business was harder to come by. Before that, Ponder was a growing force within the mercenary world. At that time, he'd leveraged his contacts to recruit close to one hundred men and had them deployed to most of the world's shitholes. Well, at least the ones where some little dictator needed some real warriors to protect him.

Looking back, he knew his expansion into protection for the Mexican drug lords had been stupid. It'd seemed so easy though. The money was ten times what the majority of security contracts were. If it weren't for that fucking Marine Colonel, he'd probably be smoking Cohibas in Antigua right about now.

It was gravy up until he got the ultimatum from one of his competitors. He still replayed the conversation in his head whenever he didn't get a contract he thought he deserved.

"Nick, this is Calvin Stokes with Stokes Security. I was wondering if you had a minute."

Ponder's head was full of cocaine sampled from his client's latest shipment. He only knew Stokes by reputation.

The guy was a former Marine and apparently a real hard-ass. "What can I do for the Marine Corps, Colonel?"

"I'm not sure how to relay this, so I'll just go ahead and say it. We've been hearing rumors that you're providing protection for the Jimenez cartel." Stokes let the accusation hang. If Ponder had been clear headed he might have handled the situation differently. He would've denied it.

"So fucking what? Even Mexicans need protection!" Ponder laughed out loud at the joke.

Col. Stokes exhaled. He'd hoped to have an intelligent conversation with Ponder. Yes, The Ponder Group was technically competition, but a certain respect was assumed between American security contractors. He'd never dealt with Ponder directly, but had heard stories of the man's exploits, both in and out of the service. The Army had drummed him out at the rank of Major after a little 'situation' in the Philippines. The unofficial report, provided by Stokes's contact at the Pentagon, gave vague details of how Ponder had singlehandedly slaughtered the families of five men suspected of being conspirators in a planned terror attack. Ponder had freely admitted to the atrocity and thrown it in his superiors' face. He even called them cowards for not doing the same.

Apparently the rumors were true, and the idiot had just admitted it.

"Look, Nick, I was just giving you a courtesy call before I turn this over to the authorities."

"What the fuck are you talking about?!" Ponder yelled into the phone.

"Without going into the details, I'll tell you that we've been doing some contract surveillance work for a Federal agency. I'm bound by our contract to give them everything I have," Stokes explained.

"Bull-fucking-shit! You're trying to torpedo my ass! I'll have your ass…"

"No, you won't." The cold menace in Stokes's voice cut through Ponder's cocaine high. "Like I said, I'm calling you out of professional courtesy. Either you wrap things up or prepare for the Feds to come down on you. It's out of my hands."

It was the one and only conversation he'd ever had with SSI's founder. He'd heard the prick died on 9/11. Asshole.

None of it mattered anymore. He was about to make his retirement. One last op and he'd be fucking rich. They might have to fend off some of the competition but that didn't matter. Ponder was on his home turf. Plus, with the promise of a king's ransom coming his way, he could afford to up his firepower a bit.

Unfolding his huge frame from the desk chair, he walked over to the large bay window overlooking his horse corral. Maybe he'd take a ride after visiting with his prisoner. It was time to make sure his little investment paid off.

CHAPTER 3

HOTEL TERRA, TETON VILLAGE
JACKSON HOLE, WYOMING
5:39PM, SEPTEMBER 26TH

Cal threw his bag on the twin bed. The room wasn't huge but more than comfortable. Outside they had a little balcony that afforded a beautiful view of the ski runs. Too bad they weren't on vacation.

"How about we go get some food."

Daniel agreed with a nod. "Where do you want to eat?"

"Let's stay close. How about that restaurant right across the quad?" Cal pointed through the window. "What does that say? The Mangy Moose Saloon? I could use a beer and a steak."

"Yeah, okay." Briggs grabbed the small backpack that Cal had recently discovered carried an assortment of reserve ammunition for his concealed weapons. Daniel took his new role as Cal's security seriously. Always the first through the door, Briggs kept a vigilant eye out for his new boss. Hell, in the first week they'd known each other he'd saved Cal's life no fewer than three times.

The two Marines walked down to the first floor and stepped outside. It was a short walk across the outdoor common area to get to the Mangy Moose Saloon. The place had an old log cabin feel and fit right into the Wyoming wilderness vibe of the trendy Teton Village development.

There weren't many patrons as they walked into the two-story establishment. Briggs paused at the door and scanned the tables. He did a once over of the Japanese couple sitting nearest the stage and the four guys dressed in riding gear sitting at the bar. No threats. Satisfied, he led the way in.

It was open seating, so Daniel chose a small table with a good view of the bar and dining area. A pretty, Nordic-looking waitress stepped up just as they were sitting down.

"What can I get for you, gentlemen?"

"Do you have any local IPA on tap?" Cal asked politely.

"Sure. Sir, what can I get for you?" she asked the blonde-headed sniper.

"I'll have a Diet Coke, please."

As the waitress walked back to get their drinks, two men walked into the restaurant and headed to the bar. Neither man looked toward Cal and Daniel, but the hair on Briggs's neck stood straight up.

They were both wearing well-worn outdoor clothing. The first man was skinny, of average height, with slicked back black hair and a wind-burned face. His beak nose was the feature that made him really stand out.

His companion was a full head taller and walked in with a swagger. He took off his grey beanie, shook out his light brown hair and sat down on the barstool.

"Give me shot of Beam." He ordered loudly enough for Daniel to hear across the room. His smaller partner quietly took a seat and ordered a beer.

Briggs didn't know the men, but he knew the type. It was the way they carried themselves. These guys were former military, and they radiated danger to the highly attuned Marine. *Wouldn't be surprised if they're armed too*, he thought.

"Don't look behind you," Briggs mentioned casually to Cal, "but I think we've got a little trouble. Two new friends just sat down at the bar."

With his back to the bar Cal couldn't see what Daniel was talking about, so he just nodded. He knew better than to question the Marine's senses. Briggs was a man of few words, so when he talked you listened. Not to mention he had an uncanny sixth sense when it came to danger. The man could sniff it out like a hound dog.

"So what's our play?" Cal asked.

"Let's just see what happens. Maybe I'm wrong."

Cal smiled and nodded.

Their drinks were served a minute later. Cal took a long pull from his large mug and savored the bitter goodness of the local beer. He'd have to ask what brand it was.

"Any movement from our friends at the bar?"

Briggs shook his head.

"You think we're good to order?"

"Yeah. Let's keep it casual. If I'm right about these guys, I don't want to tip them off," Daniel instructed.

They ordered their food and made random small talk as they ate. Cal had hoped to use the time to plan their search for Neil, but it looked like that would have to wait until later.

Finishing quickly, they asked for the check and paid. The two men at the bar were still downing their second drinks as Cal and Daniel made their way to the exit. There wasn't even a glimpse in their direction by bird nose and his companion.

Briggs hoped the warning was just in his mind. It would make their search for Patel a lot harder if they already had a tail.

"Let's take a little walk around the village and digest some of those ribs we just ate," Briggs suggested.

They headed uphill toward the large ski lift that was running the last tourists off the mountain. Both men were in excellent shape but could still feel the effects of the elevation. During their time in the Marine Corps, they'd each trained at the Mountain Warfare Training Center in Bridgeport, California. They knew it would take a couple days to acclimate to the decreased oxygen. Hopefully they wouldn't have to test their sea level legs quite yet.

After thirty minutes of walking through the modern ski village, and ducking into most of the little shops, Briggs led the way back towards the hotel. He hadn't spotted the two men from the restaurant. It didn't really surprise him. Teton Village wasn't big. It would be easy to be observed and not even know it. It would be easier to lose a tail once night fell. Darkness was already imminent.

Daniel took a right turn past a small playground, heading toward the hotel's front desk. Instead of walking into the hotel, he continued past. The darkness was almost complete as they walked by the little sushi restaurant and headed up the street toward the mountain. Briggs wanted a little free space to see if anyone was following.

Just as they rounded the corner past the last neighborhood, a set of high beams switched on and blinded the companions. They heard an old truck door open and saw a man get out and walk toward them.

"You two weren't planning on going up the mountain were you?"

Briggs could now make out the man's shape. He was wearing a Park Ranger's uniform.

Cal answered first. "No, sir. Just taking a little walk after dinner."

The young man came closer. "Just wanted to make sure. We've had a lot of bear activity up that way." He pointed up the mountain. "Bears are hungrier than usual what with the lack of berries this year."

"Lack of berries?" Cal repeated.

"Yep. This is my first year, so I don't really know the details, but the old-timers are saying the weather kept the wild berry bushes from growing enough fruit. We've even had one grizzly break into a house looking for food. Luckily the family was out of town at the time."

"Thanks for the heads-up. I think we were gonna turn around soon anyway."

They said their thanks and headed back down to the hotel. Once they were out of earshot, Cal coughed a laugh. "I almost pulled my pistol out when those lights came on."

Briggs chuckled too. "I don't think that kid knows how close he came to having his truck shot up."

Now that the tension was broken, they enjoyed the cool night air as they strolled down the hill. It was the last night of calm they'd have for the rest of the trip.

"We got eyes on the two guys. You want us to hang out?" the man with the beak nose asked his employer on the phone.

"Yeah. Get a room at Terra, and be up early so you can stick close. They'll probably start asking around about their friend. Just make sure you don't lose them," Nick Ponder instructed.

"You got it, boss."

"And, Trapper…"

"Yeah, boss?"

"Don't do anything to them until I give the okay."

The skinny man known simply as Trapper licked his lips as he thought about the coming confrontation. "I know, boss. You just let me know when."

Ponder terminated the call and sighed. He wanted to make sure his team kept tabs on all the guys SSI sent to his backyard. If he knew where they all were it would be easier to take care of them when the time came.

He'd be paying his boys overtime for around-the-clock surveillance, but it didn't matter. That would be chump change soon enough.

Ponder dreamt of his coming riches as he watched the live video of his prisoner. Patel was even now trying to hop to the small toilet in the corner of his cell. Ponder chuckled at Neil's discomfort. That leg sure had to hurt. He hoped his buyer wouldn't be too pissed that he'd had to lop the guy's foot off. It just wouldn't do to have a tracking implant around once his buyers showed up, and cutting it off had been easier than trying to dig it out.

Negotiations were still underway for the final payment amount. A small escrow of one million dollars had already been deposited into Ponder's Cayman bank account. That wouldn't even pay his mortgage on his multiple homes. No, he was in it for the big payday. Once he delivered Patel to his buyer, life would be a whole lot sweeter. Maybe it was time to ask for more money.

Nick Ponder grinned as he thought about not only the cash, but also the sweet revenge he was about to drop on Col. Stokes's company. The old man would probably roll over in his grave.

CHAPTER 4

HOTEL TERRA, TETON VILLAGE
JACKSON HOLE, WYOMING
7:17AM, SEPTEMBER 27TH

Cal and Briggs had both been up since five am, ready to start the search for their friend. After a quick workout in the hotel gym, they walked over to one of the small cafes lining the village square. Cal paid for the chocolate croissants and coffee as Briggs scanned the area for prying eyes. There were none that he could see.

"Let's eat while we walk and then get ready for the rest of the boys to get here," Cal said through a huge bite of pastry.

Returning to their room without incident, they took turns showering, and Cal checked his email. No updates from Travis.

Marine Master Sergeant Willy Trent would be arriving via private jet in the next twenty minutes. Another three SSI employees were accompanying him, including former Navy Corpsman, Brian Ramirez. Along with the four SSI operators, the Learjet was also carrying most of the gear they would need if they had to go exploring in the wild. This time of year you never really knew what kind of weather you might get. It could be bright and sunny with a high of seventy, or cold and blustery with heavy snow. Better to be prepared.

Cal had hand selected sixteen men to come along for the search. He based the selection on their prior experience with him (Trent, Briggs and Ramirez were all veterans of at least one of Cal's covert ops), and their training in mountain warfare. Cal wasn't taking any chances this time around. He also had two more teams of sixteen standing by at SSI's Tennessee headquarters if the need arose for more firepower.

Briggs walked out of the bathroom, drying his hair with a towel. "Any word from Mr. Haden?"

"Dude, I told you four times already, his name is Travis," scolded Cal.

"I know, I know. Old habits die hard, Cal. He is the CEO of our company."

"So how come you don't call me Mr. Stokes?"

"'Cause you're just a dumb grunt like me." Daniel smirked.

"Whatever," Cal returned mockingly. "No update from Trav. We're kinda dealing with a needle in the proverbial haystack."

Briggs didn't say anything as he threw the towel back in the bathroom and got dressed. "I've got an idea I wanted to run by you."

Cal looked up from his laptop. "What's that?"

"Call me crazy, but I still think those two guys from the bar last night were keeping tabs on us. I was thinking about finding them first and seeing if we couldn't...extract some information out of them."

Stokes thought about it for a minute. While he didn't doubt the sniper's abilities in the least (they called him Snake Eyes for a reason), the tiny cautious part of Cal's subconscious still wasn't sure about making a scene. "So you're sure those guys were following us? I know I don't have to tell you this, but the last thing we need is a mess right in the middle of Poshtown."

Briggs shrugged his shoulders. "You have any better ideas?"

Cal didn't, and he hated it. They were really just waiting for word from Travis before they could do anything. Apart from doing the street cop thing and knocking door-to-door, Stokes didn't really have anything better.

"Okay, tell me what you had in mind."

Trent ducked his near seven foot frame under the Learjet's exit door. He stretched to his full height as he stepped out onto the top platform of the portable steps. MSgt Trent was a black man with the muscular build of an NFL linebacker. Not only was he a professionally trained chef, Trent was also lead instructor for SSI's hand-to-hand combat training course.

"Enjoying the view, Top?" The question came from behind him.

Trent turned around to face Brian Ramirez. "Sure thing, Doc. That, and I'm trying to get the kinks out. My big ass gets a little cramped even in the nicest jets Cal puts me in."

Ramirez laughed as he and the two other SSI operators followed Trent down the stairs. In comparison, his five foot nine body fit comfortably in the luxury jet they'd just spent close to four hours on.

"I'll bet you loved spending time in AAVs," ribbed Ramirez.

"Hell no! I prefer humping to wherever I need to go, Doc."

The four SSI men gathered the gear that the airport staff was now unloading off the back of the plane. As requested, there were also four pushcarts already standing by for them to pile everything on. Within minutes, the bags and boxes were stacked neatly on their respective carts and the small team headed for the terminal.

They passed under an arch of antlers and Trent pointed up. "What the hell animal do those come from?"

"They're elk antlers. I hear they've got a big elk preserve just down the road. The Boy Scouts and some other groups go out there and pick up the antlers and give them to local craftsman. In that book I was reading about Jackson Hole they had some pictures of downtown Jackson where they've got four huge arches made out of the damn things. Pretty cool."

Trent whistled in admiration. "Can't imagine how much the things weigh." He shook his head as they continued on into the single story terminal building.

Fifteen minutes later they'd loaded all the gear into the two rented SUVs. It was a tight fit, but they'd manage to cram it all in. Trent picked up his phone and dialed Cal.

"You guys on the ground?" Cal asked.

"Yeah. We're loaded into the vehicles and headed your way. Any updates on Neil?"

"None. Travis still has the tech boys doing background checks on the people at the conference. We're trying not to alert anyone that he's missing yet."

"Good idea. I'd rather catch whoever's behind this by surprise," Trent growled. He and Neil had become close over the years. Although their backgrounds were completely different

(Neil came from a rich Indian family and Willy came from the streets of Atlanta), they both respected the other's talents and often spent their time off together. Trent couldn't wait to get his big hands on whoever was behind Neil's disappearance.

"Slight change of plans. Briggs caught a couple locals tailing us. Just to be safe, we rented a house next to Teton Village to stage everything. It'll be a little cramped with all our boys, but at least we can secure it."

It sounded like a good plan to Trent. "I call dibs on one of the real beds."

Cal was always glad to have the crusty Master Sergeant around on ops like this. He had a way of keeping things light even in the face of imminent danger.

"You got it. The new place has six bedrooms, so you can take your pick when you get here."

Cal gave him the new address, and Trent relayed the information to Ramirez to plug into the vehicle's GPS.

"See you in thirty, Cal."

Just under thirty minutes later the two SUVs pulled into the driveway of the vacation home.

"Cal sure likes to travel in style," Brian commented as he looked up at the huge single-family home.

"I think he finally realized that not spending his money wasn't an option. Besides, you know he likes to take care of his troops."

The former Corpsman nodded. It was one of the main reasons he'd accepted the invitation to join SSI. The place was like home. SSI was a group of warriors that took care of each other no matter what. That philosophy came from the very top starting with Travis Haden and Cal Stokes. They would die before seeing one of their men suffer. Their approach ensured absolute loyalty amongst SSI employees. Staff and operators were taken care of and expected to perform at the highest levels. They were an elite team dedicated to making America safer while at the same time taking care of their brothers on their left and right.

Cal lived frugally by habit. His father had done the same. Both Marines spent their time and money ensuring the well-being of their troops. One of the perks of having a highly profitable company was that Cal could fly his people first-class when appropriate and put them up in the nicest accommodations. He figured it was a very small price to pay for men who'd put their lives on the line for years and continued to do so. He could finally give back to the men who meant so much to him.

As they piled out of the vehicles, Stokes and Briggs walked out onto the second story patio.

"You guys need a hand?" Cal asked.

"You kidding? Did you not see all the shit you requested?" Trent answered in mock indignation.

Stokes grinned and headed down to the first floor to help their second group of guests unload the cold weather, hiking and mountaineering gear he'd ordered from SSI's logistics division. There wasn't much a grunt liked more than a new piece of gear.

CHAPTER 5

GRAND TETON MOUNTAIN RANGE
WYOMING
11:55AM, SEPTEMBER 27TH

Nick Ponder had yet to visit his prized guest. There was too much else to do. Coordinating his buyer's arrival had been a real pain. His contact was starting to get a little attitude about the pending acquisition. They were starting to balk at the rising purchase price. During their last conversation he'd stretched the truth by telling the guy that he had two more buyers waiting with offers. It wasn't true, but after thinking about it for a while Ponder was starting to realize the possibilities. What communist country or terror organization didn't want the brilliant mind of a resource like Neil Patel?

As he continued to mull over his options, he pulled up the latest weather report on his desktop. Shit. The updated report was calling for a huge snowstorm. He'd only been in the area for one other early winter, and it'd made the normally unflappable mercenary more than a bit uncomfortable. The remoteness of his property had its advantages, but a heavy snowfall could easily hinder his plans. If he didn't get the buyer in and out in the next day or two, they might have to wait another week. He needed to buy some time. Luckily, he had a couple contingency plans.

He logged into one of his many email accounts and composed a message that would remain waiting in the drafts folder for the only other person who knew of the account's existence.

———◆———

Terrence Zheng took another gulp from his Diet Red Bull. The higher ups at SSI had him doing triple work since Neil's disappearance. He had barely stopped for the last two days.

Taking a quick break from the background check he knew would be fruitless, Zheng got up from his chair and walked to the restroom. He stepped into the large handicap stall, sat down on the toilet and pulled out his smart phone. Tapping on the appropriate application, he opened the browser and clicked on a bookmark labeled 'Vacation.' The email provider's website popped up a second later and he logged in.

There was a message waiting for him in the Draft folder.

CHAPTER 6

They now had three quarters of their sixteen-man team sitting around the large dining room table. Cal had ordered pizza and everyone was eating their fill. Briggs had just run them through the plan he'd devised to flush out the bad guys.

The last team arriving was led by one of Cal's new go-to guys. He was a short Hispanic who everyone called Gaucho. Eccentric in his own way, the small Mexican-American wore a braided goatee and commanded his men with flair and daring. As a former Delta commando, Gaucho was no novice to covert operations. He was the first man to volunteer to accompany the expedition despite his dislike of the cold environment.

Gaucho's group of four was even now pulling into the quiet ski village. They'd be at the rental house any minute.

"Hey, Cal, make sure we save a couple pieces of that jalapeño pizza for Gaucho. You know what'll happen if you don't," MSgt Trent joked to the room. The men laughed because they knew it was true. Gaucho was the first one to make fun of himself and his ancestry, but beware to the person that got in the way of him and spicy food. Despite the gravity of the situation, Stokes always enjoyed being with these men. There wasn't a guy present that wouldn't give his life for another. It was a hard thing to find outside of the military.

"So, is everyone good with Daniel's plan?" Cal asked.

Everyone nodded. Briggs knew what he was doing. Besides, the plan only entailed finding and possibly capturing two guys. It was a stroll in the park for these operators.

⬥

Gaucho and the last three team members pulled into the long driveway twenty minutes later. It didn't take Cal long to brief the newcomers and get them something to eat.

"Thanks for saving me some jalapeños, Boss," Gaucho said through a mouthful of greasy pizza.

"You're just lucky I didn't put Top in charge of the pizza," Cal quipped.

"You messin' with my pizza, Willy?"

Trent waived his hands in mock fright. "No way, hombre! You know I wouldn't get in between a Mexican and his hot peppers."

"Very funny, Top. I could say the same thing about you and some fried chicken," the small Hispanic smiled.

"Now don't be talkin' about Mama's fried chicken. Besides, I don't just eat fried chicken, I eat HOT chicken," Trent added, rubbing his six pack abs.

"That's right I forgot about that. Some spicy shit, right? You sure you don't have some Mexican in you, Top?"

"Not that I know of, brother. But who knows, maybe you're a brother from another mother." Trent smiled wide, walked over to Gaucho and gave him a big bear hug.

The tough little Hispanic wiggled out of the giant's arms and just managed to save his slice of pizza from falling on the ground. "Okay, Willy. I know how you boys in the Marine Corps like to hug but save that for Doc over there."

Looking up from his bag, Brian Ramirez gave Gaucho the finger.

"Whoa, whoa, watch where you stick that thing, Doc. I'm here for business not a medical exam." Gaucho was now snickering along with some of the other men.

"All right, ladies," Cal raised his hands in surrender. "As much as I'd love to see where this thing ends up, let's get all the gear staged. I just got a weather update from HQ and it looks like we've got a big snowstorm moving in. The cold weather gear we brought along might be coming in handy sooner than we thought."

Gaucho groaned. "You're kidding me right, Boss? You know how much us Mexicans hate the cold."

"Really? Why don't you just hitch a ride on Top's back? I'm sure he can keep you warm," Cal offered innocently.

The remark elicited a middle-fingered salute from the former Delta man and MSgt Trent.

———

"What have you got for me?" Nick Ponder asked Trapper.

"They haven't left the hotel. I'm thinking they gave us the slip."

Ponder's temper flared. The last thing he needed right now was an enemy force snooping around in his territory.

"So what are you doing to find them?"

"We got their room number from our contact at the hotel. We're about to go take a look inside."

"Call me as soon as you know."

Ponder slammed the phone down. He was losing precious time. The snowstorm was really constricting his timeline. Pretty soon he'd have to recall his men. He only had a handful of contractors working security at his home base. He'd need the full contingent for the buyer's arrival and to deal with any possible incursion from the SSI team. Maybe it was time to trigger his back-up plan.

After consulting his small journal, he picked up the secure phone again and dialed a number. It connected after one ring.

"Yeah?"

"Jack, I need a favor."

CHAPTER 7

CAMP SPARTAN
ARRINGTON, TN
3:46PM CST, SEPTEMBER 27TH

Travis Haden was on the phone when Marjorie "The Hammer" Haines, SSI's lead attorney, walked into his office. Wearing her usual form-fitting office attire, Haines was always impeccably dressed in clothing that enhanced her already attractive form. Most people underestimated the beautiful brunette. Not only was she a lion in the courtroom, The Hammer was also an accomplished martial artist. She'd bested many of the toughest of SSI's operators in practice sessions or wager-inspired sparring.

She motioned for him to end the call. After apologizing to the caller, he hung up the phone.

"What's up?" Haden asked with concern. It wasn't often that Haines came into his office unannounced.

"We've got a little…situation. I just got a call from my source at the FBI. It looks like they're about to conduct a little *unofficial* investigation on us."

Travis frowned. It's wasn't that he'd never expected the request. Hell, after the Black Knight affair a few years ago most of the security contracting companies had been investigated in some form or fashion. SSI had thus far avoided the FBI's scrutiny by maintaining the proper transparency and cultivating the relationships needed to keep the company out of hot water.

What concerned Travis was SSI's covert wing. They'd operated outside the laws for years, protecting a country that still seemed unaware of their presence. Living and breathing their founder's concept of *Corps Justice*, SSI quietly intercepted threats that normal law enforcement couldn't handle. Each operation could only be sanctioned by Travis or Cal. Secrecy was key.

Had someone tipped-off the FBI? Cal had only recently saved the President's life in an operation in Las Vegas. They'd worked directly with the President and the Secret Service to keep the entire affair quiet but that didn't mean anything. Somehow secrets always got out. It was directly proportional to how many people actually knew the secret. The Vegas incident was still fresh. Did the President have a turn of conscience?

"Do you have any details?"

Haines shook her head. "Nothing yet. My contact says we should be getting the subpoena within the hour."

"Shit. This couldn't have happened at a worse time. Where will they start?"

"From what I heard from some friends, they'll start digging into finances and operations. They want to make sure income and expenses match."

"Is there any way they can trace us back to any of our clandestine ops?"

"I don't think so…at least not on paper." The look on Haines' face told Travis she was holding something back. He gave her a 'give it to me' hand gesture.

"I didn't want to say anything until I had a chance to think about it more, but I'm concerned that we've got a mole." She let the comment sink in. Marge could see by the look on Haden's face that he found the idea pretty far-fetched.

"You're kidding, right?"

"Think about, Travis. Neil gets kidnapped then not days later we have the FBI breathing down our necks. That can't just be coincidence."

Travis didn't know what to think. Ninety plus percent of the employees at SSI were former Military personnel. They'd each been exhaustively vetted mentally, physically, financially and through intense background checks.

"Okay. Let's assume you're right. What do we do now?"

"While I deal with the FBI, have Higgins and Dunn start doing an internal search."

Dr. Alvin Higgins was a former CIA employee and psychologist. Despite his chubby appearance and jolly charisma, the good doctor was a master interrogator. He'd revolutionized the techniques used by American personnel (both physical and chemical) that now produced tomes of vital intelligence for the American government. Although he abhorred most physical violence, Higgins marveled at the capacity and the inner workings of the human mind. If there was a man that could extract information without laying a finger on a captive, it was Dr. Higgins.

Todd Dunn was SSI's head of security. Where Higgins was outgoing and genial, Dunn was introspective and serious. A former Army Ranger, Dunn was all about business and always vigilant.

Travis nodded. If anyone knew how to be discrete it was Higgins. Tag teaming with the burly Dunn, the two would find the mole soon. "What are you gonna tell the FBI about where Neil, Cal and the rest of his team are?"

Haines shrugged and smiled. "I'll let you know as soon as I know."

―――――――◆―――――――

Within twenty minutes Dr. Higgins was executing his plan. They'd talked about the possibility of having a traitor in their midst before. Luckily, thanks to Higgins's experience in the federal government where mole hunts seemed all too common, SSI had a plan in place for just such a scenario.

"I'll take care of it, Travis," Higgins said in his fatherly tone.

"You'll let me know what you find out right, Doc?"

"Certainly, my boy. Just give me little bit of time. These things have a way of working themselves out."

Travis wasn't too sure. Since his time with the SEALs he'd become accustomed to working in an elite environment. Amongst warriors it was absolutely unspeakable to betray your brother's trust. That gave Haden an idea.

"Hey, Doc, how about you start with the support staff. Most of our operators don't even have a clue about what's going on outside their current mission. Might save us some time and heartache."

Even though he'd already come to the same conclusion, Dr. Higgins was never one to take credit or condescend. "Good idea, Travis. I'll start there."

As Travis left the doctor to his craft and went to find Dunn, he could only hope that the internal investigation wouldn't tear his company apart.

CHAPTER 8

TETON VILLAGE
JACKSON HOLE, WYOMING
3:15PM, SEPTEMBER 27TH

Cal walked into the garage where his men were busy staging their equipment. Some checked weapons as others ensured their cold weather gear fit properly.

"Top, you got a minute?"

MSgt Trent looked up from his conversation. By the look on Cal's face he knew another wrinkle had just been added. Trent nodded and followed Stokes upstairs.

Ramirez, Briggs and Gaucho were already seated around the dining room table. Trent took a seat while Cal remained standing.

"I just got a call from Travis. It looks like they're having their own little party back at headquarters. The FBI's about to investigate SSI."

To their credit, the men seated around the table remained silent. They knew it wasn't time for questions.

"Travis and The Hammer aren't sure what they're looking for but I agree with them that it's mighty convenient

36

considering Neil's disappearance. What makes things worse is it also looks like there might be a mole at SSI."

Now the gathered warriors looked shocked. Could it be? Could one of their own actually be conspiring to destroy a company they'd all fought hard to build?

Trent was the first to interject. "How sure are we about this, Cal? I mean, this could be bad for all of us."

"I know. Trav has Higgins and Dunn on it. If anyone can ferret this guy out it's them."

They all nodded solemnly. Each man was well aware of Higgins's expertise.

"So how does this affect what we're doing out here?" Gaucho asked, seeming almost nonplussed about the situation back home.

"As usual we'll have to make sure we stay under the radar. I've also recommended to Travis that he keep all updates I send him to his immediate leadership team. No one else really needs to know about what we're doing," Cal explained.

"What if we need more firepower, Cal?" asked Ramirez.

"I think we need to try and get this done without asking for more people. Besides, if what they're saying about this snowstorm is true, we wouldn't be able to fly anything in anyway."

These men were all used to working on their own. They knew the risks involved. Not having the ability to call in support would not hinder them from seeing the mission through. They would make do.

"Cal, I know we shouldn't be thinking this," Trent started, "but have you considered that maybe Neil isn't even here? I mean, what if they flew him out of here the second they picked him up?"

"I've discussed that with Travis and we're both in agreement that it's the risk we have to take. We don't have anything else to go off of. Besides, if Daniel's right and some unknown group is out there watching us, that probably means it's worth it for them to keep tabs on us. I don't think they'd do that if he was already shipped overseas."

Trent wasn't so sure, but he didn't disagree. They all had to hope that they could reach their friend in time.

———

Neil rubbed his sore leg for maybe the thousandth time. The pain was getting worse, which meant his captors would be bringing him his pain meds soon. He'd kept a mental time clock since waking in the small cell. At regular intervals a large man with a black mask would silently open the door, place a plate of food along with two pills on the floor just inside the room. There was no need to worry about the prisoner attacking the guard. Without the use of his foot he was effectively immobilized.

After the first delivery, Patel had refused to eat the food or take the medicine. An hour later his jailer had returned as Neil lay shivering and pain-wracked on his small cot. The large man forced Neil's mouth open with one hand and shoved the two pills down his throat with the other. It was impossible for Patel to resist.

Within minutes the pain had receded. Neil had learned his lesson. Take the pills or live in excruciating pain.

As he counted down to his next meal, Neil thought about his friends. He knew they'd be out looking for him. Would there be any clues left to find?

Deep down he knew it was his fault. For years Travis and Todd Dunn had hounded him about taking along security when he went into public. They'd said he was too valuable an asset to lose. Cal had one day said he was, in fact, a prime asset. He'd always shrugged off the worry. As fate would have it, his father had once been kidnapped and murdered while travelling on business overseas. Would he endure the same fate? Something told Neil that wasn't the case. They had something in mind for him. Why else would they go through all the trouble of taking care of him?

He wracked his brain thinking of possible ways he could escape, or at least figure out what they wanted from him. Neil knew they would tell him soon. His sixth sense told him it wouldn't be pleasant.

Upstairs Nick Ponder went over the latest email from his buyers. They'd accepted his counteroffer with some conditions. The mercenary was ecstatic. Pretty soon he'd be rich and never have to worry about petty little jobs again. But first he had to have a little talk with his prisoner. It looked like the buyers wanted to run a test to see that they were getting what they paid for.

Ponder cracked his knuckles as he thought about the coming session. It would be good to be rich again.

Neil's cell door opened and a huge man with a shaggy black beard and shaved head walked in. Patel knew the boss had arrived.

"You and I need to have a little chat, Mr. Patel," Nick Ponder growled in baritone.

"Is this where you tell me I get to go home now?"

Instead of answering, Ponder walked across the small space, grabbed a handful of Neil's hair with his left hand and clamped his right hand around Patel's neck and started to squeeze. With barely any effort, he lifted the smaller man off the cot and up against the wall.

"Now you listen here, you little shit. I'm someone you don't want to fuck with. If you're looking for God, I'm him. I could squeeze the life out of your pathetic little raghead body right now."

Patel didn't doubt the man. No longer able to breathe, he fought to maintain his consciousness. This guy was incredibly strong.

Without warning, Ponder dropped Neil back on the small cot. Patel screamed as his stump hit the floor. His captor laughed.

"Like I was saying, I am God to you now. Whatever I say, you do. Understand?"

Through gritted teeth and watery eyes Neil nodded. He didn't have much of a choice. Even at full strength he was no match against the large man.

"I'll be back in a couple hours with some things for you to do. Get your mind right, and you might leave here in one piece."

Without another word Ponder left the room. Neil was left to wonder what the sadistic man had in mind.

CHAPTER 9

"Everybody ready to go?" Cal asked the sixteen men. Needing to blend in, they were all attired in varied hiking and casual clothing. Each man carried a small arsenal under his coat. Cal had his trusted double-edged blade strapped to his left wrist along with a pistol in his waistband.

They'd agreed that Cal and Trent would be the bait. The Mangy Moose restaurant had an outdoor seating area where the two Marines would grab a table and have a leisurely dinner. Briggs was certain that the enemy would find them soon in the small ski village.

The small teams set off at staggered intervals. Some left in groups of four, others left in groups of two or three. Briggs was the only man to go out alone. The sniper they called Snake Eyes was already making himself comfortable across the quad on the pool deck at Hotel Terra. It afforded a full view of the common area. All the other teams would take up

41

positions at various points in and around the Mangy Moose. The only thing left to do now was wait.

Trapper and his partner sat at the outdoor restaurant attached to the large ski lift. They'd searched Cal's hotel room earlier in the day and found it completely empty. Ponder had already recalled the other contractors because of the storm. That left Trapper to coordinate the search in Teton Village.

The wiry man kicked himself for not taking out the two Marines when he'd had the chance. It would've been so easy that first night. Now it seemed that his quarry was on to them. To make matters worse, the rest of the sixteen man team Ponder's guys had already confirmed landing at the Jackson Hole airport had also disappeared. Trapper wished someone had listened to him when he'd suggested putting a couple tails on the arrivals after they left the airport. Ponder was so confident that the SSI men would start the search in Teton Village that he'd ignored the suggestion.

Trapper was a veteran of the Army's military police. He'd gained his nickname by being able to track and trap anyone. There wasn't a man or woman that he couldn't find. The only reason he hadn't stayed in the Army was the 'questionable' methods in which Trapper had used to detain his captives. In the end, there had been allegations of abuse and torture. While Trapper knew they could never prove anything (he was also a master at manipulating evidence and witnesses) he felt the writing was on the wall. Certain senior officers had made it their patriotic duty to see him drummed out of the service.

Instead of going out their way, Trapper decided to take early retirement at sixteen years and head to the civilian world. Not long after he'd contacted his old friend Nick Ponder. They'd partied over booze and drugs, all the while lamenting the Army's decline as a military force. The next morning over Bloody Maries, Ponder offered him a job with what he'd affectionately dubbed 'Ponder's Misfits.' It didn't take Trapper long to find out that the majority of contractors hired by the Ponder Group were indeed misfits. Released from active duty for an assortment of reasons, Ponder snatched them up willingly knowing that they had nowhere else to go. As a result, they were only too happy to do his dirty work.

Trapper glanced at his watch. "Five more minutes, and let's take a walk around."

His partner nodded silently and finished his coffee. Trapper paid the waitress and minutes later the two men were strolling downhill doing a surveillance sweep toward The Mangy Moose.

————

Briggs spotted the two men right away. It was hard to forget their mismatched faces. They looked completely nonchalant as they walked down towards Cal and Trent.

Daniel pulled out his cell phone and texted the rest of the team: *2 TARGETS HEADED TO THE MOOSE*.

Once he got confirmation from the team leaders, he slipped the phone back in his pocket and stood up. It was time to see who these guys were. He slipped out of the pool deck quietly and headed to the stairwell.

———◆———

Trapper spotted Stokes and Trent as soon as The Mangy Moose came into view. He nudged his partner. The man looked up and nodded. At least they'd found them again. Now it was time to take up a position and watch.

The two contractors veered to the right and found a spot on one of the outdoor tables maybe a hundred yards away. Trapper casually pulled out a pack of cigarettes and sat down. While he wished there were more people around, at least the darkness would give them some cover. Stokes, on the other hand, was sitting in a well-lit area that afforded Trapper a perfect view.

He and his partner were so intent on their targets that they never noticed Briggs watching them from behind.

———◆———

Daniel extracted the two pistols from his voluminous coat pockets. He'd have to make his shots count. It was something the sniper was used to. Briggs never missed.

———◆———

As Trapper took another drag off his cigarette, he sensed movement to his left. He turned to look and felt a stabbing pain in his neck. He reached up, grabbed the dart and yanked it out while staggering to his feet. His partner was doing the same. Trapper had just enough time to register that it was Briggs approaching when he fell to the ground. The powerful tranquilizer quickly rendered both men unconscious.

Daniel rushed to check on them and waived for the other team members to come help. Four SSI men materialized out of the darkness and swiftly picked up the two men and carried them to a waiting vehicle.

Briggs was scanning the area to make sure nothing was left behind when an older couple walked up concerned.

"Excuse me, son, but is everything okay with your friends over there?" the old woman asked.

"Yes, Ma'am," Daniel answered politely. "My buddies just had a little too much to drink over at the Moose."

The husband smiled knowingly. "You tell them to take it easy on the booze at this altitude. Had a bad go of it myself a few years ago."

"Yes, sir, I will. You have a nice night."

Briggs walked away and breathed a sigh of relief. His silly little plan had worked. Now it was time to find out what these guys knew.

CHAPTER 10

They'd put the two men in separate rooms. Briggs had recommended they start with the big guy first.

Cal had disagreed. "I really think we should start with the guy with the beak nose, Daniel."

"Don't ask me why, but I get the feeling that he's gonna be a hard nut to crack. It's something in the guy's eyes."

Cal knew better than to question the sniper's judgment. In the short time he'd known Briggs, the Marine had never been wrong. "Okay, let's do it your way. What did you have in mind?"

Lance Upshaw wasn't a bad man. He just wasn't the brightest guy that ever walked the Earth. What he lacked in mental ability he more than made up for in strength and skill. Since his first day in the Marine Corps even his drill instructors had taken to calling him 'The Swede' after the character in Clint Eastwood classic *Heartbreak Ridge*. Upshaw had excelled in all physical aspects of boot camp. He'd continued his growth training in the fleet. His large athletic frame, honed from years on the football and baseball field was perfect for the Marine Corps. It was his ability to be manipulated that became his final downfall.

They'd given him an Other Than Honorable discharge from the Marine Corps because of a certain hazing incident he'd been convinced to participate in. Upshaw's fire team leader, a skinny sadist named Cpl. Kliner, had taken offense to the 'tone' of one of his new PFCs. The kid was a college drop-out who'd instantly incurred Kliner's wrath. After a few drinks at the Enlisted Club on Camp Pendleton, and under Kliner's direction, Upshaw methodically beat the young 'college boy' within an inch of his life.

Something in Upshaw knew that what he'd done was wrong, but it had been an order from his fire team leader. Wasn't he supposed to follow orders? That's what his DIs had said at Parris Island.

Upshaw remembered sitting in the courtroom in complete shock as the officer read his sentence. How could the Marine Corps send him away for following orders? He loved the Corps.

Sitting in his cell months later, he'd welcomed the visit from Nick Ponder. The man understood his situation and even admitted going through a similar episode years ago. Once Lance served his year in the brig, he happily took a position with The Ponder Group. After all, they knew what it was like to be misunderstood.

Lance Upshaw shook his head as he regained consciousness. He didn't remember how he'd ended up in the room.

Where the hell am I? His arms and legs were hogtied behind the wooden chair someone had strapped him to. He couldn't feel his hands and feet.

As his vision cleared, he finally made out a figure standing in front of him. The man was around six feet in height with a blonde ponytail. Lance thought that he had kind eyes. Despite his lack of brainpower, Lance knew the difference. He'd seen evil in many of the men he'd met in jail.

Daniel pulled up a chair and sat down in front of the large captive. "What's your name?"

Upshaw wasn't sure he should respond. He remembered something from boot camp about only giving out your name, rank and serial number. "Upshaw, Lance. Seven, three, three, two, nine, eight, one, two, one."

"So you were in the Army?" Briggs asked kindly.

Upshaw made an almost disgusted face. "Marine Corps." Briggs smiled. "Me too."

Upshaw didn't say anything. He'd learned to keep his mouth shut. Daniel let the silence linger. This guy looked liked a perfect candidate to handle a medium machine gun but would never be found planning a raid. He had the hard look of an abused animal.

"Look, I'm a little short on time so I'm just gonna get to it. That cool?" Daniel asked.

Upshaw still didn't know what to say. The last thing he remembered was sitting next to Trapper and watching the guys Ponder had sent them after. He was just the muscle sent along to help his partner with any heavy lifting. He'd always been told to not saying anything in the event he was captured or questioned.

"I'm not gonna hurt you, Lance, but I need to know what you and your pal were doing following us."

Options swirled in Lance's head. He knew Trapper and Ponder would kill him if he said anything.

"I'm not supposed to say."

Daniel wasn't surprised by the response but happy that he'd at least validated his initial impression. These guys were on SSI's tail. Without saying another word, he got up from his chair and went to find Cal.

———

Nick Ponder was starting to think it'd been a bad idea to send his guys to watch the crew from SSI. He'd known there was always the chance they might be spotted. That's why he'd sent Trapper. The guy was a one-man surveillance machine and mean as a snake. He was Ponder's kind of guy.

He tried calling Trapper's cell phone for a fourth time. Sometimes the signal was crappy up in the mountains. He figured the gathering storm wouldn't help much either.

For the fourth time Ponder got the error message trying to connect to Trapper's phone.

"Shit," he grumbled.

Half of his men were already back. He'd need to bring the rest home soon. The helo wouldn't be able to fly in the coming blizzard.

Where the hell were Trapper and Upshaw?

———

Trapper regained consciousness slowly. He looked around the room then tested his arms and legs. They were bound behind the dining room chair he was sitting on. The former military policeman was pretty sure he could get out of the restraints as long as he could force some blood flow back into his limbs. There were benefits to being somewhat of a contortionist. The problem was he didn't know what he was up against. He was sure his captors would make an appearance soon enough. Meanwhile, he'd bide his time, work his arms and legs, and figure a way out.

"This guy's not the smartest is he?" Cal asked Daniel as he continued to watch the live video feed from both holding rooms.

Daniel shrugged. "He's smart enough to keep his trap shut. At least we know they were keeping an eye on us. You okay with me laying into him a little more?"

Cal looked up from the video screen. "If it gets us closer to Neil, do it. I'd prefer not leaving any marks on these guys…"

"I don't think it'll come to that. I'll be subtle."

"Do what you need to."

Daniel nodded and headed back in to talk to Upshaw.

Daniel took his seat in front of Upshaw and stared at the man for a minute. To his credit, Upshaw returned the stare without flinching.

"Where are you from, Lance?"

Upshaw hesitated. He didn't remember anything about not talking about his personal life. There couldn't be anything wrong with that, right?

"I'm, uh, from Dallas."

"You play football down there?"

Upshaw's eyes lit up at once. "I did," he said with pride and almost puffed out his chest before remembering that he was tied to a chair.

"Thought so. I'll bet you tore it up on the field. Linebacker?"

"Running back," Upshaw said with a grin.

"Really? You're a pretty big dude to be dodging tackles."

"I'm fast, and I can run over most guys."

Briggs whistled in admiration. He would honestly love to see the man in action.

"You play college ball?" Daniel asked, already knowing the answer.

"Nah. Didn't have the grades."

"So you went in the Corps instead."

Upshaw nodded his head. Although it'd taken some studying with his recruiter, he'd finally passed the military aptitude test and was allowed to go to Parris Island.

"So when did you get out of the Corps?"

Lance scrunched his face thinking. Numbers and timelines sometimes got jumbled in his head. His mother always said that God could only give a person so many gifts and that Lance had gotten a lion's share of physical ability. In exchange, God couldn't give him as much intelligence as other kids his age.

"I think a couple years ago."

"What did you do after you got out?" Daniel asked.

Upshaw hesitated again. His mind tried to process whether answering would be right or wrong. It was hard to keep it straight.

"Went home for a little bit."

"Just hung out with your family?"

"My ma raised me as a single mom. I hadn't seen her in, like, a year. Stayed with her for a while."

Briggs could feel the walls coming down. "Did you get a job down in Dallas?"

Upshaw shook his head. "No. I just helped Ma and some of her friends. Got free food and a place to sleep."

Daniel nodded thoughtfully. He didn't want to have the guy clam up again. It was important to get him to keep answering questions. Briggs said a silent prayer that God would guide him to the answer.

"Your mom still live down in Dallas?"

"Yeah."

"You still see her?"

"I fly down one or two times every year."

"She pay for your flight?"

It was another one of those funny questions Lance wasn't sure about. Why was he asking?

"Um…no. I pay for my tickets."

"Oh! So do you have a job up here?"

"Yeah."

Briggs noticed the drop in Upshaw's demeanor. He had to keep it light.

"Cool. It must be pretty awesome living up here. It's beautiful."

Lance nodded as enthusiastically as a little kid. "You should see it when the leaves change. It's really pretty. All the moose and bears come out too. I like the bears."

"You ever see one?" Briggs asked with eyes wide open.

"All the time! Right now they're really coming out. People are saying they're more hungry than other years."

"That's what I heard too. You ever get charged by a bear?"

Upshaw was suddenly serious. Briggs thought that maybe he'd gone too far and delved into a memory that would end the man's cooperation.

"Just one time. Damn grizzly was huge. We were hiking back down to Phelps Lake and all of a sudden this bear was just sitting in the middle of the path soaking up some rays. I tried to scare it away, but it got up and roared at us. Before we knew it the thing was charging."

"Holy crap! Was your buddy in the next room with you?"

"Nah. Trapper was back at HQ. I was with some of the other guys."

"So what did you guys do?"

"The only thing we could do. We shot the fucking thing!"

Daniel whistled again. "Wow. Did you kill it?"

"Damn right. It was him or us."

"Can't you get in trouble for killing a grizzly around here?"

"Yeah, but we didn't stick around. Would've moved it but those things weigh a ton."

"I'll bet. So you work with some other guys at one of the ranches around here?"

"Yeah, sort of," Lance answered quietly.

"So you do guided hikes, trail rides, that sort of thing?"

Upshaw hesitated again. He'd already made one decision in his mind: that this guy asking him questions was actually a nice guy. Lance didn't think he'd tell his boss if he said anything.

"No, we do some security work."

"Really, that's cool. I kinda do the same thing. Who'd you say you worked for?"

"I…uh…didn't."

"Yeah, but wouldn't it be easier if I talked to your boss about all this instead of bugging you? The sooner you tell me where you work, the sooner I can give them a call and get his whole thing straightened out. You seem like a good guy, Lance. I don't want you to get in trouble."

Trouble was the last thing that Lance wanted. What could it hurt? As long as they didn't say anything about him telling.

"You promise you won't tell them I told you?"

"I give you my word as a Marine, Lance."

That was good enough for Upshaw. "I work for The Ponder Group."

CHAPTER 11

Travis hadn't left the office since Neil disappeared. He'd commandeered one of the large suites at The Lodge so he could stay close by. The phone on the bedside table rang just as he dozed off for a quick nap.

"Haden."

"Sir, I have a call for you from Mr. Stokes," the operator said.

"Patch him through, please."

Luckily, all the phones at The Lodge were highly encrypted and therefore highly secure. With the number of VIPs SSI courted, it was important to have a way for guests to communicate with their offices while away. It was one of the many improvements Neil Patel had instituted over the years.

"You there, Trav?"

"Yeah. What's going on?"

"You ever heard of some company called The Ponder Group?"

Haden sat up in bed. "Yeah, why?"

"We've had a tail since we got here, and we just found out that they work for this Ponder Group."

"How do you know?"

Cal hesitated. Even though the line was supposedly secure, he still wanted to be careful just in case someone was listening.

"Let's just say we have two more guests at the house."

"Invited or uninvited?" Travis asked.

"They were...invited. Daniel made it a...personal invitation."

Travis correctly deduced that they'd somehow apprehended the men.

"Tell me you've used kid gloves on the guys."

"You know me, cuz, always trying to do things the right way."

"I'm not messing around here, Cal. Tell me you didn't put the screws to these guys."

Cal laughed at his cousin's unease. "Of course not. Briggs just had a little chat with one of our new buddies. So you wanna tell me who this Ponder Group is?"

Travis swept his hand back through his dirty blonde hair. Where to start?

"SSI has a little history with The Ponder Group," Travis started disgustedly.

"What kind of history?"

"The CEO of The Ponder Group is a prick named Nick Ponder. The guy is former Army. Mean son-of-a-bitch. He's as crooked as they come. So anyway, back in the nineties, he and your dad..."

Travis told Cal the story of the conflict between Cal Sr. and Nick Ponder.

"How come you never told me about this?" Cal asked indignantly.

"There was never a need to. It happened a long time ago. I've heard rumors about him over the years, but he knows to stay clear of us."

"Looks like that's not the case anymore."

"Yeah. The only good thing I can think of in this whole situation is that Ponder is just a thug. He likes money and inflicting pain and not much else."

Cal was fuming. He didn't know how his cousin could stay so calm. "I'm having a hard time understanding what in the hell you're talking about. While we're sitting here chatting about this asshole, he's probably torturing or even killing Neil!"

Travis took a slow breath. "Look, now that we know WHO has Neil, we can actually do something."

Cal knew his cousin was right. A couple hours ago they had nothing. Now they had a name.

"How can we find out where this guy lives?" Cal asked.

"Let me call you back. With a possible leak here at home I'd rather take care of this myself. I'll do some digging and get you the details in a few minutes."

It wasn't good enough for Cal, but he wisely held his tongue. Venting his frustration on Travis wouldn't accomplish a thing. He needed to focus on one thing: Nick Ponder.

———◆———

Travis hung up the phone and stared at the wall. Where to start? He hesitated using any of the computer guys until he knew where the leak was. There was always the Council of

Patriots, an ultra-secret group of retired (and one active) politicians. Typically, the Council came to SSI for help in going operational on intel. This was a different story. Travis had never contacted the Council for help. He'd put that on hold for now.

He picked up his cell phone and speed-dialed his head of security, Todd Dunn.

"Dunn," answered the former Ranger in his gruff tone.

"Todd, I need to talk to you in person."

Travis could hear Dunn getting up from whatever chair he'd just been sitting in. Once set in motion, Todd Dunn was never moved off track.

"What's up?"

"Cal just found out that Neil might have been taken by an old friend."

"Who?"

"Nick Ponder."

"I'll be right up."

Travis placed his phone back on the bed and looked up at the ceiling. It was going to be a very long night.

CHAPTER 12

Daniel hadn't gotten anything else out of Lance. It had prob-ably finally sunk in the large man's brain that he'd divulged a little too much information.

"You want me to go talk to the other guy?" Briggs asked Cal.

Cal had already told the rest of the team to get some rest. They might have to leave soon, and he wanted them to get any sleep they could. It was one of the many things he'd learned in the Marine Corps: sleep whenever and wherever you can.

"Let me go see if I can get anything out of him. I'm start-ing to think you were right, though. Looks like a tough nut. Wish we had Doctor Higgins with us. He can make anyone talk."

"Just be careful, Cal. He's tied up pretty good but don't take any chances. You want me to come in with you?"

"Nah. Why don't you just watch the monitor. If anything happens, you can come to my rescue." It was meant as a joke,

59

but neither man was laughing. As men of action, they felt stifled. Better to be moving than to remain static. Without the information on Ponder's whereabouts, they couldn't do a damn thing.

Daniel took a seat in front of the video display and settled in to watch.

———◆———

Cal stepped into the second holding room and closed the door. He looked at his captive. The man looked bored.

Ignoring the look, Cal grabbed a chair, positioned it six feet from his prisoner and sat down.

"So, Trapper, you wanna tell me what your deal is?"

Trapper seethed inside. Apparently Lance had opened his big fucking mouth. He'd have a little talk with the dumb shit soon.

Instead of answering the question, Trapper started laughing. It started off as a chuckle and escalated from there. Soon, the man was almost convulsing with laughter.

This guy's a lunatic, Cal thought. He glanced up to the camera and shrugged at Briggs.

Soon, Trapper settled down and sat taking in brief breaths of air between giggles.

"What's so funny, Trapper?" Cal asked, not amused.

"Ha…ha…ha!…You…you're…funny…" Trapper spit out in the middle of girlish snickering.

His patience already thin, Cal stood up from his chair. "How about you shut your fucking mouth before I shut it for you," he growled.

The order fell on deaf ears. Trapper went back to howling like a madman. Cal just stood and watched. He couldn't do anything with this guy. Hopefully Travis would call back soon with something they could act on.

"Have it your way, buddy. Laugh all you want. You've got two choices: either help us out or get thrown in a deep dark cell somewhere."

This caused another riotous uproar from the beak-nosed man.

Cal shook his head and turned to leave.

"Wait…wait…I want to…tell you something," Trapper just managed to get out.

Cal turned back. "What do you want to tell me?"

"A…a secret."

Wary, Cal stepped closer to the man but still kept his distance. He would've felt better with a baseball bat in his hand. "What is it?"

"Come…closer…hee hee," Trapper coughed as he threw his head back again.

"No way. Tell me your secret."

Trapper's head snapped down and his gaze steadied on Cal.

"There's a third option," Trapper responded clearly.

Cal's blood froze and the hairs on the back of his neck stood up. Just as he reached for his pistol, Trapper somehow, impossibly, spread his legs that were no longer tied, and hoisted the chair over his head. Cal went to block the coming swing but instead of hitting him, Trapper continued his swing and launched the heavy chair at the oversized bedroom window. The skinny man followed the chair's trajectory. With hands and feet now free, he ran the short distance to the window and jumped.

Instead of shooting with his drawn pistol, Cal stood shocked. He didn't really want to fire his pistol in the small residential community. The cops would come running. A split second later, Cal was jumping out the window too.

———

Daniel had been watching the interaction closely. He knew something was up Trapper's sleeve, but the man hid it well. Almost the same instant that the crafty captive stood up from his chair, Daniel was doing the same thing. With his pistol extended, he bolted for the bedroom door.

———

Trapper hit the yard with his feet and immediately went into a roll to lessen the impact. His teeth still rattled as he sprang up and sprinted away from the house. He needed to get in touch with Nick Ponder.

———

Cal landed less gracefully than his quarry. He thudded painfully and fell forward. Luckily they'd jumped onto the grassy yard instead of the concrete driveway barely four feet away.

Only steps ahead, Trapper was moving in high gear as Cal struggled to regain his balance. The guy was moving incredibly fast. Cal chided himself for not checking the man's restraints. It was a basic rule in handling prisoners.

Pocketing his pistol in case they encountered neighbors, Cal ran after Trapper.

Daniel skidded to a halt at the bedroom window and stuck his head out. He could see Cal running into the darkness. Without another thought, Daniel avoided the broken glass, climbed onto the window frame and jumped. Hitting the grass, he rolled out gracefully and hopped into a sprint. He took off after the two men hoping he wouldn't be too late.

There weren't many places for Trapper to go. The terrain was pretty open. Luckily it was pitch black out. He was free, but for how long? He'd chased countless criminals on foot so he knew the pursuit was all about tenacity and the wits of the man being chased. His mind processed the landscape and alternative routes. The neighborhood would end soon.

Trapper turned left on McCollister Drive, running up the incline. The only chance he had was using the clumps of trees on the slopes as cover. He knew exactly where to go.

Cal was lagging behind. Not a bad athlete in his own right, Cal was no match for Trapper's speed. The only reason he could still see his former detainee was because the guy had stayed on the well lit road. Cal was sure that wouldn't last long. He'd glimpsed Daniel coming up from behind but couldn't wait for his friend.

He pushed his legs and lungs to their limit. Neil's life depended on it.

Trapper hit the tree line and smiled. Unless his pursuer had somehow managed to grab a set of night vision goggles or a hound dog to sniff him out, there was no way he was getting caught.

Trapper looked back once, then disappeared into the woods.

Cal saw Trapper glance back just as Daniel caught up. Both men extracted their pistols and rushed forward. They ran in silence knowing that their chances of catching the man had just decreased exponentially.

Daniel stopped Cal as they approached the tree line. "Let me go first," the sniper ordered.

Cal would've ignored most other men but knew Daniel's skills outweighed his own when it came to the cat and mouse game they were playing with Trapper.

Without waiting for his employer to reply, Daniel melted into the wooded area.

After thirty minutes of looking, the two Marines emerged. The only thing Cal had to mark the occasion was a slightly sprained ankle and a variety of scrapes on his face. Daniel, on the other hand, looked clean and composed. How was it that he never seemed to get scathed?

"Thanks for coming after me," Cal offered.

"Sorry we didn't get the guy."

"It's my fault. I should've checked him," grumbled Cal.

"I'll bet if we look back at the video we won't even see how he got out of those restraints. That guy's a real pro."

Cal simply nodded. Just when he thought things might be going their way, it had gotten worse.

"Shit."

Daniel looked at Cal with serene confidence. "We'll get Neil back. Don't worry." He patted Stokes on the shoulder twice and started walking.

Cal stared back at his friend. For some reason he believed him. There was something in Daniel that inspired trust and calm. He'd talked about it with Trent a couple days before. MSgt Trent, being a much more spiritual man than Cal, thought that Daniel had some kind of God-given gift. He tried explaining it to Cal.

"I knew a preacher when I was a kid. Momma always said he was blessed by Jesus. This dude would walk into crack houses and gang hangouts and somehow come out untouched. He had this calming presence that good people flocked to and that bad people respected and were scared of. It's hard to explain other than to say that your boy Daniel has the same thing. Have you ever seen the kid get hurt or angry?"

Cal had not. He remembered the story Daniel had told him about his last time in Afghanistan. After the SEAL team they'd accompanied got killed by a large insurgent group, a building collapsed on him and his spotter. His spotter died and Daniel walked away unscathed except for the mental scars. After leaving the Marine Corps and wandering aimlessly through alcohol and bad dreams, Briggs found God. He never talked about it, but you could almost feel the invisible bond the former sniper held with the Almighty.

He looked over at Daniel as they walked back to their house. Briggs walked with an air of confidence that most men wished for. Cal hoped that Daniel's gift would help them find and rescue their lost friend.

CHAPTER 13

It hadn't been hard to lose his pursuers. Trapper knew the area well, and the dark night further aided his escape. He paused again to catch his breath and listen for sounds of pursuit. Nothing.

The safe house wasn't far. Just another ten minutes of jogging and he'd be there. Trapper took off down the dirt path. There was a storm looming on the horizon, and it had nothing to do with the weather. The killer's mind imagined the retribution he'd soon levy against Cal Stokes and his men.

Cal and Daniel returned to the house and awakened the team. Two men were posted to guard their remaining prisoner. They wouldn't lose this one.

After reviewing the taped interrogation two more times, they agreed that it was very likely that The Ponder Group had at least a base of operations if not a headquarters in the area. The assumption was confirmed minutes later by a call from Todd Dunn.

Cal had a pen and paper out, ready to take notes as he talked to SSI's security head.

"I've confirmed that Ponder registered his corporation in Wyoming. He's got a P.O. Box listed in the public record along with his attorney's address. The lawyer's office is in Wilson, which is just around the corner from Teton Village. I'm still working on locating his physical address."

"Sure would be nice to have Neil around right now," Cal noted ruefully.

"Yeah, he would've found Ponder in a couple minutes."

"Any progress on finding out who the leak is?"

"I think we're getting close. Me and Higgins narrowed it down to five guys in the R&D department. Neil hired them all. Looks like they didn't get as thorough a check as most new hires do."

"How did that happen?" Cal was confused about the security lapse by the otherwise overly cautious Dunn.

Dunn exhaled. "I won't blame it on Neil, but I'll probably have to have a little talk with him if we get him back."

"WHEN we get him back," Cal corrected.

"Right. WHEN we get him back, Neil needs to have a little class on security. We all know he's prone to seeing the good in people. Looks like this time it's really coming back to bite him in the ass."

"That seems a little harsh, Todd."

"I know it might, but we wouldn't be in this mess if it weren't for Neil. Shit, Cal, you know I love him as much as you and Travis do, but Neil really messed up on this one.

First he denies the personal security and now we're finding out that he probably hired a rat. I think it's time for a little wakeup call for Mr. Patel."

Cal knew Dunn was right. He could only imagine how bad Neil's wakeup call was going.

Neil was in the process of learning another lesson at the moment. He'd refused to do the 'test' Ponder had demanded. Now, for the third time, Neil was stripped naked and tied to a post outside the compound. The first time had been a warning. The second time lasted longer. This time Neil was sure he was almost hypothermic.

The temperature had to be in the low thirties. To make matters worse, every five minutes Ponder would walk outside with a bucket of cold water and dump it on the shivering Patel. Neil would cower and try to make himself and small as possible. He had no idea how long this time would last.

He kept himself going by thinking about his friends: Cal, Trent and Brian. Neil knew they wouldn't back down. He'd seen the after effects when they'd finally rescued Cal from the gangster Dante West. His friend came out beaten and bloody but in good spirits and, more importantly, alive.

Neil vaguely remembered MSgt Trent telling him that it was all about toughness and humor in the beginning. First get pissed off, then make it funny. *Didn't Senator McCain say the same thing?*

Neil knew that eventually all men broke under torture. He had to hold out as long as possible. The alternative was simply too terrifying to think about. If he used his talents to do what his captor wanted, he knew where it would lead. They were testing him. Patel was simply a tool to be used.

Despite his time with the company, he never truly understood the dangers their elite warriors faced. He'd heard the stories from the sidelines of the action, but being in the thick of it was something else entirely.

The front door of the low building opened and light spilled out into the darkness. Ponder's form appeared with his now familiar metal bucket.

"You ready to take your test or do you want to take another bath?" Ponder asked.

From his position on the ground Neil thought once more about his friends. *What would Trent say?* Between chattering teeth he answered. "I thought you'd…never ask. I was getting…hot out…here."

Ponder walked faster and threw the water right in Neil's face. It jolted him and took his breath away. Whatever reprieve Neil expected disappeared a second later when Ponder bent down and put his face right in front of Patel's.

"Now you listen here. I can do this shit all night. You'll feel like you're about to die and then we'll bring you back to life."

He reached down and grabbed Neil bandaged stump. Neil clenched his teeth as Ponder began to squeeze.

"Come on, you pussy. You know you want to scream. Go ahead, no one can hear you anyway." Ponder squeezed harder and harder as Neil struggled to stay lucid. Tears streamed down his face as he turned to his aggressor.

"You're…the….pussy."

Ponder yelled in his face and followed it up with a quick head butt. Neil crumpled into unconsciousness.

"Shit," muttered Ponder. He hadn't meant to knock the kid out. Time was running out and so was his patience. The buyers were hounding him about providing proof that Patel was the real deal. Add the snowstorm blowing in and Ponder was scrambling to keep the transaction together.

He fished out a walkie talkie from his coat pocket. "Come out here and get him."

Thirty seconds later, the hooded jailer walked out, unlocked Neil from the pole, and picked him up gently.

"Put him back in his cell and warm him up. We'll try again in the morning," Ponder ordered.

The jailer nodded and carried his package back into the building.

Ponder stood outside, marveling at the stars. The view was crystal clear. It would be gone tomorrow when the clouds rolled in. He hoped it wasn't a sign of things to come. There was too much riding on the sale.

Neil regained consciousness just as he was being laid back down on his cot. He pretended to still be unconscious as the guard covered him with a blanket and left to fetch the large electric heater they used to bring Neil's body temperature back to normal.

Shivering under the wool blanket, Neil had one more thought as he drifted off into a fitful sleep. *I won this round, asshole.*

CHAPTER 14

Dr. Higgins and Todd Dunn were looking over the files of the five suspects. All five were relatively recent hires. Only one had been at the company for longer than a year. They were similar in that they all had some kind of computer science background. Under Neil Patel's leadership, SSI's R&D division had grown quickly over the preceding years. Cyber attacks were becoming more and more frequent around the globe, and Neil wanted to be part of the force fighting it.

The year before, the U.S. military's new Cyber Command had enlisted SSI's aid in building a more secure infrastructure. They now had SSI on retainer for future consultation with the caveat that Neil Patel be the lead troubleshooter.

"Do we still have all of these men on the premises?" asked Higgins.

"Yep. I gave the whole division orders to stay close a couple days ago. They're effectively on lockdown working around the clock."

"Good. They're probably nearing exhaustion. That should help our interrogation."

"What do you want me to do, Doc?" Dunn knew a thing or two about questioning suspects, but he also understood that Dr. Higgins's skills were on a whole other level. The pudgy professor was the most effective interrogator Dunn had ever witnessed. You don't get to be the CIA leading expert on interrogation techniques without having a lot of success. Higgins had paid his dues around the globe countless times.

"I'd like for you to be with me for the questioning. Do you think you can play bad cop?"

Dunn offered a rare smile. "No problem, Doc."

Higgins went back to the files.

"I know I don't have to tell you this, Doc, but we need to find the leak fast and have time to assess the full extent of the damage. Marge says the federal investigators are coming tomorrow."

Higgins looked up from his scanning. "Then I guess we better get to work then."

Dunn shook his head in amusement. Leave it to Higgins to state the obvious.

———

Thirty minutes later they'd devised their plan. Dunn picked up the office phone and dialed his deputy's number.

"I need four guards to meet me at the Batcave now. Tell them to come loaded." The Batcave was what everyone called Patel's underground research and IT facility. It not only held multiple office suites full of computers, but it also housed a large warehouse area that the teams used to test new technology. As a joke, someone had even plastered a few *Batman* movie posters on the door leading into the cavernous main room.

He hung up the phone and looked at Higgins. "You ready to go?"

"After you, Todd."

———•———

Five minutes later, Dunn and Higgins linked up with the four-man team waiting at the security desk outside the R&D labs. Each man wore all black combat suits and carried an H&K G36C automatic carbine. The fire team leader nodded to Dunn, who motioned for the men to follow.

The six men walked quickly down the long hallway leading to the entrance of the Batcave. Dunn put his hand on the entry scanner, and a second later the heavy magnetic lock clicked open.

Grabbing the door handle, Dunn turned to the fire-team leader. "Take Dr. Higgins down to the interrogation rooms. Help him setup whatever he needs. I'll be down in ten minutes."

SSI kept 'mock' interrogation rooms in the depths of its Tennessee campus. Used mostly for training, the rooms were now being utilized for the first time ever on SSI's own employees. It still shocked Dunn that a breach of this magnitude happened on his watch. He promised himself that it would never happen again.

As the four operators escorted Higgins to the lower level, Dunn headed to the common computing room that most of the geeks occupied after hours. He'd already confirmed with security that the five men he wanted to question were still there.

He walked into the large common room and looked around. Even though he'd never been to the headquarters of Google or Facebook, this is what he imagined it probably looked like. The room was huge and wide open. There were dartboards and a ping-pong table in one corner and a full array of video game systems in another. The center of the space housed modern tables of varying shapes and sizes. Twenty some odd programmers and technicians were scattered around the room engaged in both work and play. Dunn understood the necessity to blow off steam, especially if you spent all hours underground. The guys worked hard and deserved the added amenities.

Scanning the large room, he quickly found the group he was looking for. They were clicking away on mini laptops. Everyone was so engaged that they didn't even turn as Dunn moved closer. One young man finally looked up. "Can I help you, Mr. Dunn?" The caution was evident in his tone. Todd Dunn was known throughout SSI for his no B.S. attitude. If he came calling, you stood at attention. The rest of the small gaggle took the hint and stopped what they were doing.

"I need to see some of you." Dunn read off the names. "If you can close up whatever you're working on and meet me in the next room in five minutes, I'd appreciate it."

Without another word, Dunn turned around and left the room.

"I wonder what that's all about," commented one of the programmers.

No one bothered to answer the statement. The five employees called out by Dunn quickly packed up their gear.

Terrence Zheng tried to hide his discomfort. He'd been one of the five Dunn had requested. Zheng tried to act casual as his nerves rattled inside. The last thing he wanted to do was spend time with Dunn. He'd thought that the FBI investigation would've given him the opportunity to leave the campus unnoticed, but there hadn't been a chance to yet. Not only was his division being worked overtime, it had also been discretely recommended that they all remain on the headquarters' grounds.

Terrence had to somehow get word to Ponder that they were starting to question employees. Maybe his newest benefactor could get him out of it.

As the five men stepped out in the corridor Zheng spoke up.

"Hey, can you tell Dunn that I'll be there in a minute? I've gotta hit the bathroom. Too many Red Bulls," Zheng offered embarrassedly.

"You better hurry up," answered a small Vietnamese named Tony. "I heard the last time someone kept Dunn waiting he made him strip down and do push-ups in the cafeteria cooler."

Zheng gave Tony an exasperated look as the others laughed. "I'll be there in a second."

He walked quickly to the restroom and headed for the nearest stall. Sitting down to relieve himself, Zheng pulled out his cell phone and logged in to the remote email server. He wrote a quick note and left it in the drafts folder. Flushing the toilet, he hoped the entire ordeal would be over soon. He looked forward to a much-needed vacation on a beautiful island.

EPISODE 2

CHAPTER 15

Terrence Zheng left the restroom and joined the others.

"Sorry about that, Mr. Dunn. Figured I should take a piss before we got started," Zheng offered.

Todd Dunn nodded. "We're headed downstairs. There've been some developments in Neil's disappearance but we need your help. It shouldn't take long."

They all looked at Dunn in confusion. Usually they were allowed to work independently. Initial guidance was given followed by the occasional check-in. Then again, the current situation was unique. They all knew Neil well as he'd hired each one of them. The overtime they'd logged wasn't just mandatory, every man had volunteered to stay and work.

Zheng played along because everyone else had. He couldn't wait to walk out that door and never look back.

Dunn continued, "We're trying to nail down details so we can find out what happened. I know you've probably already answered some of this stuff but me and Doc Higgins wanted to hear it personally."

Two of the men groaned. What had already looked like a long night just got longer.

Dunn ignored the frustrated sighs, then turned and headed to the stairwell. As he walked, he was already running the interrogation through his mind. He'd already chosen his first target: Terrence Zheng.

The mood went south as soon as they reached their destination. Even though they were used to working in the subterranean facility, this was something else. The main waiting area held stadium seating similar to what you might find in a university or outside an operating room in a teaching hospital. Everything had the sterile feel of a medical facility too. There were no decorations or even the slightest attempt to warm the place up. It was what it was, an interrogation facility.

The seating overlooked ten rooms, each about twelve by twelve with a metal table and two sets of chairs. Although the lighting was comfortable in the gallery, the interrogation rooms looked like they were lit by prison spot lights.

None of the five had ever been to the interrogation pod. There were only a handful of SSI employees that had the security access to come this far underground.

SSI's head of security didn't try to lighten the mood. This was exactly what he wanted. He needed them to be on edge. They were visibly uncomfortable. Dunn directed the suspects to leave their belongings on a table in the middle of the room. They were then searched from head to toe by one of the guards and escorted to separate rooms.

As the five men entered their respective space, Dunn stepped into a side room that housed the control room. One wall was comprised of flat panel screens displaying video of each of the ten rooms. Dr. Higgins was sitting in one of the comfortable leather couches, reviewing his files one last time. He looked up as Dunn walked in.

"Everything go well with the roundup?" he asked cheerfully.

Dunn nodded. "They didn't freak out until we walked into the gallery."

"That's to be expected. I can only imagine what is going through their heads at this very moment."

"I think I know who we should start with. This Zheng kid." Dunn pointed at the screen broadcasting Terrence Zheng in high definition. "Something doesn't feel right about him."

"Anything tangible?"

"Not that I can put my finger on, but there's something in his eyes. It just looks like he's hiding something."

Higgins pulled out Zheng's file.

"Let's see. Terrence Zheng, born April 3rd, 1989 in Burbank, California. Parents are from Beijing, China. He attended the University of California at Berkeley for under-grad. Graduated with honors in three years and double-majored in Computer Science and Electrical Engineering. Went to MIT for graduate school. Dropped out after his first year to run a start-up. Won a spot in SSI's business mentoring program. His company was sold last year for a tidy sum, and Zheng was then hired by SSI. He is now part of our cyber-security team and is tasked with monitoring our network and preventing intrusion.

"I must say, Todd, if this is our man, we might have quite a predicament on our hands."

Dunn sighed. All but one of the five suspects worked in some critical capacity at SSI. He didn't even want to think about the possible calamity should SSI's network be laid bare.

"You have any problem with me playing the bad cop?" Dunn asked.

"I was rather hoping you would."

Zheng looked up at the mirrored observation window. It was even brighter in the room than it had seemed from the observation deck. He was uncomfortable but tried to act calm as he waited for someone to begin the questioning.

Todd Dunn and Dr. Higgins entered. Higgins took a seat while Dunn leaned against the opposite wall. The muscular man's calm demeanor was gone. It felt like Dunn was staring a hole right through him. Despite his thought to do otherwise, Zheng began to sweat.

Dr. Higgins started. "Hello, Terrence, my name is Dr. Higgins." He reached across and shook Zheng's hand warmly. "I'm sorry we've taken you away from your work but we had some pressing questions to ask you and your colleagues."

"Anything I can do to help, Doctor," Zheng offered as cheerfully as he could.

Higgins smiled. He could feel the nervousness rolling off of the young man. It wasn't unusual even for innocent men to feel uncomfortable in such surroundings. Through the years Dr. Higgins had developed a highly accurate barometer for judging people's innocence. It usually only took a little friendly banter for Higgins to deduce whether a suspect was, in fact, hiding something. Getting the person to divulge the information was something else entirely.

"I appreciate your help, Terrence. Now, as you know, we've lost one of our most important assets, Neil Patel. We'd like to ask you some questions to see if we've possibly missed something. Sometimes in these investigations it's the smallest, most mundane detail that solves the case."

Zheng nodded gravely.

"How long have you known Neil?"

"Uhh, I'd say a little over two years."

"You were one of the recipients of our start-up funding, were you not?" Higgins asked.

"Yes. I started a company called PlanBot. It was essentially cloud-based planning software."

Higgins glanced down at the file. "Ah yes, and it says here that you later sold the company."

"That's right. With SSI's help we found a larger company that wanted our technology."

"Fantastic! You must have been very excited." Higgins smiled.

"It was a lot of fun. I couldn't have done it without you guys, and Neil, of course."

Higgins paused again and pretended to go through the file. He had already memorized the key points and merely used the time to form his next line of questioning.

"So after you sold your company, you decided to come work at SSI. Was there a reason you didn't go into, what do they call it nowadays…early retirement?"

"Honestly, I considered it. I made enough money that it would've been easy to find a place and settle down."

"So what made you come to work here?"

"I really enjoyed working with the guys when I was in the start-up pipeline. There was always the opportunity to start something new again but this seemed like a good challenge. After a couple conversations with Neil, he offered me a job."

Higgins knew he was being told the truth. Not only did he sense it, he'd taken a similar path after working with SSI on a particularly challenging assignment during his tenure with the CIA. The caliber of individual and the high degree of integrity impressed Higgins immensely and ultimately led to his retirement from government service. He'd never looked back. It was a common story amongst SSI employees. Here they were valued.

"How do you like it now that you've been here for a bit?"

Zheng hesitated. He knew this was where he had to be careful. "It's been good."

Higgins caught the hesitation. Was it simply a matter of an employee being unsatisfied with his work or was there more?

"Let me rephrase the question. Do you feel like you've been challenged professionally since you've been here?"

After a brief pause, Zheng answered. "At first I don't think Neil knew where to put me. To be honest, some of the stuff he had me working on was pretty basic. Once he had a better idea of my capabilities he started giving me more and more."

It sounded reasonable. After all, Zheng was used to running his own company. Former business owners didn't always turn out to be the best employees. Going from a world where you make all the decisions to having someone else telling you what to do wasn't always easy.

"And how is your relationship with Neil?"

"I think it's pretty good. He doesn't really micromanage so I mainly just see him in staff meetings."

"Did you know about the conference Neil was attending in Wyoming?"

Zheng hesitated for the briefest of moments. *Here it comes*, he thought. It didn't matter. They couldn't trace a thing to him unless Ponder gave him up. He knew that would never happen. Plus, he'd covered his tracks like a true professional.

"Sure. We all knew he was going out there. I think someone even bought him a cowboy hat as a joke."

Higgins chuckled. "I think I heard about that. Did you know what the conference was for?"

"I'm not sure. Neil mentioned it was some VIP thing. I did hear that he was giving a class or maybe a lecture."

Zheng began to relax. Maybe they really were just ironing out the details. Deep down he enjoyed this game of cat and mouse. He'd played it for years online. There'd been a few close calls in his early days of hacking, but he hadn't come close to being caught in a while. This was the first time he'd experienced the adrenaline rush of a face-to-face confrontation. The excitement played through his body as he secretly savored the moment. He was better than them.

"Did he mention where he was staying in Wyoming?" Higgins asked.

"I'm not sure. I know he was in Jackson Hole, but I didn't have the details." In truth, Terrence Zheng knew all the details. Neil was never very careful about hiding anything from his staff. Zheng had Neil's entire itinerary memorized. He'd even pulled up the Google Earth image of Hotel Terra during the time he knew Neil was being kidnapped. What he wouldn't have paid to see the look on the cocky bastard's face.

"Did you know that Neil refused to take any personal security on the trip?"

Zheng did. "I think he mentioned something about that. Neil doesn't seem like a big fan of being escorted around."

As the suspect finished his answer, one of the guards walked in and handed something to Dunn. Trying to looking nonchalant, Zheng glanced their way. *That's my phone!* For a split second Zheng panicked. He quickly calmed, though, knowing there was no way they could get past the encryption he'd installed. If they tried, the phone would effectively cease to work. He knew how to cover his tracks.

After a few whispered words, the guard left and Dunn turned his attention back to the questioning. Higgins twisted around in his chair and looked at Dunn. "Any updates?"

Dunn nodded, walked to the table and raised Zheng's phone. "You wanna tell me what you were doing with your phone in the bathroom?"

"I was just checking my email."

"Anything interesting?" Dunn asked with a raised eyebrow.

"Not really."

"Let's cut the crap, Terrence. Tell me what you were doing with your phone," Dunn ordered.

Zheng stood his ground. "I told you, I had to take a leak and out of habit I checked my email. I might've gone on Facebook too, I don't know."

Dunn looked his suspect right in the eye. "Tell me how you know Nick Ponder."

Zheng's eyes dilated rapidly, but he caught himself before panicking. "I don't know..."

There wasn't time to finish. Faster than Zheng thought possible, Dunn came around the table, grabbed him by the neck and pinned him against the wall.

The smaller man struggled. He didn't know how to respond. Unaccustomed to physical violence, Zheng pissed his pants as Dunn squeezed harder.

"I'll ask you again, how do you know Nick Ponder?" he loosened his grasp just enough for Zheng to croak back.

"I...don't..."

"Wrong answer, asshole." Without warning, Dunn smacked him across the face. "Now tell me how you know Nick Ponder!"

Zheng looked to Dr. Higgins for help. To his surprise, the jolly doctor sat placidly. He actually looked like he was enjoying the exchange.

"You...can't...do..."

Dunn answered with another slap that brought tears to Zheng's eyes. "I can do whatever I want, you little traitor. Now you listen to me. What I'm doing right now is child's play compared to what the Doc over there can do to you. You either answer me now or I let him have you."

Zheng's mind couldn't comprehend what was happening. There were laws. He had rights. They couldn't torture him, could they? His mind was clouding and he didn't know how to respond. He wasn't prepared for this.

"But...I don't..."

Dunn answered the unfinished statement by slamming his forehead into Zheng's nose. Bone and cartilage cracked as the small man crumpled to the ground and fell into unconsciousness.

Ponder was still awake monitoring the deteriorating weather and hoping he wouldn't get another message from his buyer. He'd have to get more creative with Patel. There was just too much riding on the transaction.

He opened up another tab on his internet browser and logged in to the email account he shared with Terrence Zheng. The last he'd heard from Zheng was that SSI was preparing for the FBI audit by working them overtime. Ponder didn't care about how much the little Asian worked. He wanted to make sure they weren't on his trail yet. After selling Neil, he didn't give a shit who knew. Ponder would be long gone by then. Until that happened he might have to tie up some loose ends, like Terrence Zheng. The kid had been useful in getting Patel's travel itinerary and giving him a heads-up about the teams that followed, but ultimately he was a liability. Ponder figured he'd probably have Zheng killed as a precaution. He'd done it before. The thought of killing another human was more a necessity for Ponder than a crime.

His internet connection was slow, so he waiting impatiently for the email server to load. Finally coming up on his screen, Ponder clicked on the Drafts folder. There was a message from Zheng.

PRIME ASSET

My presence requested with four others by Dunn. I'll let you know when I'm finished.

Ponder froze. The message was casual only because the little shit didn't know who he was dealing with. Ponder knew Todd Dunn only by reputation. The former Ranger was regarded throughout the industry as a thorough operator. Dunn never cracked under pressure. He was as solid as they came.

Maybe there was a chance that they were still safe. Ponder quickly discarded the thought. He had to plan for the worst. Just as he was mulling over his options, his cell phone rang. He didn't recognize the number but only a limited number of people knew where to reach him.

"Hello?"

"It's me."

Trapper!

"Where the hell have you been?"

"I'm at our house in the village."

Ponder knew that meant Trapper was at their little safe house in Teton Village.

"What are you doing there?"

"We ran into a little distraction," Trapper answered cryptically, always cautious about using even secure phones.

The hairs on the back of Ponder's neck rose. "What kind of distraction?"

"Those friends we were looking out for invited us in for a little talk. I had to leave Lance so I could let you know."

"How bad is it?" he asked.

"I think you're about to have company."

He gripped his cell phone to the point of breaking it. Nothing was going according to plan. It was time to salvage the situation.

"Can you get back here?"

"Not quickly."

"What if I arrange a helo?"

"Sure."

"Okay. I'll call you back."

Ponder ended the call and looked at Neil Patel's sleeping form in the small video window of his computer screen. "Your friends aren't gonna fuck this up for me."

He picked up another phone and dialed the afterhours line for a helicopter pilot that owed him a few favors. Ponder had saved the guy's helicopter company from creditors. In exchange, The Ponder Group had free use of the company's helo.

After four rings the man picked up in a groggy voice. "Yeah?"

"It's Ponder. I need you to fly one of my guys from Teton Village over to my place."

"Can't this wait until tomorrow?"

"No, it can't. Now get your ass out of bed. My guy will be calling in a few minutes."

Ponder slammed the phone down, picked up his cell phone and dialed the number Trapper had called from. He quickly gave his employee the phone number for the company owner and told him to get back as soon as possible. He'd need all the manpower he could get.

"Hey, boss, why don't we just bug out for a while? We can take your new friend and get out of town."

"I'm not running away. We'll deal with these guys once and for all."

Trapper knew better than to try to dissuade him. Once he made his mind up, that was it.

"Just don't do anything until I get there, okay?" Trapper requested.

"Then hurry your ass up!"

Ponder threw his phone across the room where it crashed into the far wall and smashed into a hundred pieces. He calmed enough to think about the looming conflict. Part of him wanted to get the sale over with and leave. The fighter in him wanted to stick around and deal with the SSI problem. Maybe he could do both.

Grabbing another thick cigar, Ponder mentally ran through his options. He'd often dreamt about defending his castle against invading hordes. It looked like this might be his chance.

CHAPTER 16

CAMP SPARTAN

ARRINGTON, TN

2:36AM CST, SEPTEMBER 28TH

When Terrence Zheng finally awoke, he found himself strapped to a hospital gurney. His arms and legs were secured with Velcro restraints. He tried to lift his head and almost screamed in pain. His face throbbed from the vicious head butt administered by Todd Dunn. Zheng took a couple steadying breaths and looked up slowly.

They'd moved him into another room. It was similar to the first but as he looked around, Zheng saw a variety of medical equipment neatly arranged on two wheeled tables. Next to the tables were three IV stands.

"I see you're awake, Terrence," Dr. Higgins's voice came over the speaker system. "I'll be right in."

Part of Zheng hoped it was all a bad dream. Maybe the FBI or even Nick Ponder would come running through the door and rescue him. He let his mind wander until Higgins entered through the room's only door. He was attired in black scrubs and almost looked like a contestant on *Top Chef* except for the face shield he had propped on the top of his head.

"I'm sorry about Mr. Dunn's little transgression. I got you cleaned up as best I could."

"That man is a lunatic! When I get out of here…"

"Shhh," Higgins ordered with a finger to his lips. "You might want to watch what you say. Mr. Dunn is still listening." He pointed to the one-way window.

"But I haven't done anything wrong!"

Higgins shook his head as if disappointed.

"We both know that's not true, Terrence."

"You don't know…"

"Oh but I will, Terrence," Higgins replied with an almost embarrassed shrug. "Do you know what I do at SSI, Terrence?"

"You…uh…you're a shrink or something."

"That's partially true. While my job does require me to attend to the mental well-being of SSI employees, my background is actually in interrogation."

Zheng strained to look back at the doctor.

"Oh, I'm sorry. How rude of me." Dr. Higgins moved to the side of the gurney and reached underneath. Something clicked and Zheng flinched as he heard the electric hum. The stretcher slowly tilted forward so that he was no longer lying flat.

"Is that better?" Higgins asked.

Zheng nodded through fear-filled eyes.

"So, as I was saying, my background is in interrogation. I rather hate the word but it is quite accurate." Dr. Higgins adjusted his glasses as he walked over to one of the IV stands.

"You see, I spent the first part of my career with the Central Intelligence Agency. When they wanted someone to talk, they flew me in. You can't imagine how many countries I've been too. Now, I only tell you this so that we might save time."

"What...what do you mean?"

"One way or another you will tell us what we want to know. Most people think they can resist divulging the truth. I think it's because they watch too many movies. Well, that's simply not true. Everyone talks. It's just a matter of when."

Zheng couldn't believe what he was hearing. He'd seen the chubby doctor around the campus on many occasions. Higgins looked more like a jolly uncle than what he'd just described. He was always chatting with SSI employees and telling the latest jokes he'd heard. Zheng just couldn't get it through his head that there could be any other reality.

"Doctor, I really don't know what I'm doing here. I work on the computer systems and that's it. I'm not even..."

He realized Higgins wasn't listening. Instead, he was preparing the various IVs and instruments, and moving them closer to the gurney. Dr. Higgins finally turned back to Zheng.

"I've been working on a very special recipe. I haven't had a chance to try it out on a human subject, so this will be perfect timing."

Zheng's eyes went wide as Higgins swabbed his arm and inserted the IV needle. "Now, this won't hurt as long as you don't struggle. Allow the drugs to work their way into your system." He turned the dial on the IV, and Zheng felt the cold flow of liquid entering his blood stream.

"I'll let that run for a few minutes, and then I'll be back in to talk to you."

"Don't leave me in here!" Zheng screamed in panic.

Higgins ignored the outburst and left the room to consult with Dunn. He was sure they'd have their answers soon.

"Have you found anything on his phone?" Dr. Higgins asked Dunn.

"No. I've got one of the other computer guys taking a look at it now. Looks like Mr. Zheng might have loaded it with some extra security features."

Higgins had expected as much. This new breed of youth was comfortable manipulating technology. Besides, he wasn't sure they'd get any more out of the phone than through the interrogation.

"I'll give him ten minutes and the solution should be fully in his system. Is there anything else you'd like me to ask?"

"Just what we discussed before. I need to get Cal as much intel as I can. There's a big snowstorm about to blow into Wyoming, so we need to work fast."

"I always do, my boy."

"We do need to figure out what to do with the kid once we're done questioning him."

SSI had never had to put away any of its own employees before. It wasn't possible to just dump him on the local police department. Zheng knew too much. Dunn also didn't want to kill the guy. They weren't murderers.

"Let me see if I can make a call to some of my old friends at the Agency. I'm sure they can find a space for our friend in one of their maximum security cells."

Dunn liked the idea. If they could pull a few strings, Zheng would never see the light of day again. It's what he deserved for selling out Neil and the company.

"Go ahead and do that. In the meantime, we'll hold him here until this whole thing with Neil gets resolved."

Higgins agreed and left the room to make the phone call. Dunn looked into Zheng's holding room. *We better get some answers soon.*

———•———

Dr. Higgins strolled back into Zheng's room, this time with the face shield down. You never knew when someone might like to spit in your face.

"How are you feeling, Terrence?"

Zheng couldn't respond for a moment. He'd been surprised to find that no pain accompanied the IV's injection. In fact, instead of feeling worse, he almost felt euphoric.

"I'm feeling pretty damn good, Doctor!"

Higgins smiled warmly. He never knew why some interrogators insisted on administering pain to make suspects talk. Through the miracle of modern medicine, there were now easier ways. Over the years, Higgins had learned to manipulate men with the use of a variety of intoxicating tools. He'd learned to vary his doses based on not only the physical characteristics of the subject, but also their temperament. Like an expert anesthesia practitioner, Higgins knew exactly how to manipulate the body to get a desired effect. He felt it was better to have a compliant and happy subject, and mixed his drugs accordingly. Let them gnash and scream later. His job was to find the answer in the quickest and most humane way possible.

"I'm glad you're feeling better, Terrence. Now, are you ready to answer some of my questions?"

A small part of Zheng screamed alarm, but the thought was swiftly pushed aside by the swirl of the potent drug. "I'm happy to help in any way I can," he answered.

"Good. Let's start with some easy questions, shall we?"

Zheng nodded eagerly. For some reason he had an overwhelming urge to help. He wanted to tell the truth. The real story of his life felt like it was going to burst out of his lungs. Why had he been so defensive earlier? Dr. Higgins only wanted to help him, right?

"First, your name is Terrence Zheng, correct?"

"Yes, but my friends call me Z."

"Ah. You don't mind if I still call your Terrence, do you?"

"Nope."

"How long have you worked for SSI, Terrence?"

"I think for about a year."

"And what is it you do at SSI?"

"I help maintain the company's network security."

"Do you do any work for our clients?"

"I've done some consulting with the Department of Defense."

"And what was the nature of the consulting?"

"They're trying to beef up their new Cyber Command. If you ask me, they're way behind the power curve."

"What do you mean, Terrence?"

Zheng laughed out loud. "I could out-hack any of those guys."

"So you're a hacker, Terrence?"

"Yeah, I've been breaking into stuff since I was a kid."

"I assume it always came easy for you?"

"Yeah. I think the first time I hacked into someone's computer was when I was, like, eight years old. My dad wouldn't let me play games on his PC, so I learned how to break in."

"How would you rate your skills as compared to your peers?"

Zheng thought about his answer. He wanted to be as precise as he could for the kind doctor. "I'm not saying I'm the best in the world. The best guys spend all their time hacking. I'm more of a part-timer."

Higgins had a hunch he wanted to work out. "How would you say your skills compare to say…Neil Patel?"

Zheng's face scrunched up, and then he smiled proudly. "I'm better."

Higgins wasn't so sure. He'd heard from numerous friends that Patel could possibly be one of the world's elite computer geniuses. He hadn't heard of a single system Neil couldn't break into. Higgins was starting to feel that Zheng had a highly inflated opinion of himself. Was that a possible motive? He'd be testing the potency of his drug mixture, but Higgins was all about experimentation.

"Why do you feel you're better than Neil?"

"I'm younger and I know the newest ways to get around things," Zheng stated.

"So you feel that you could do Neil's job better than he does?"

Warning bells once again sounded in the recesses of Zheng's mind. Was he supposed to answer that question? As before, the drugs swept away any doubt.

"I definitely think I can do the job better."

It was time to ask the most damning question. Higgins was now sure that the young man would answer truthfully. Although he wanted the answer, he still dreaded it.

"Is that why you helped Nick Ponder kidnap Neil?"

Zheng answered without hesitating. "Yes."

CHAPTER 17

After almost an hour of questioning, Dunn and Higgins felt like they had everything they needed. Zheng's motive had been power. He didn't really need the money. Even though Zheng was set to make a pretty penny from Ponder, it was the possibility of taking down a man like Neil that had truly motivated him. For him it was a challenge similar to breaking into his father's computer the first time.

Dunn cursed the young upstart for his stupidity.

"How long will he be doped up like that, Doc?" Dunn asked.

"He should be coming out of it soon. Do you think what we learned will help get Neil back?"

"The biggest thing we needed was to confirm that Ponder was behind it. That guy is a real piece of work. If the FBI wasn't coming tomorrow, I'd be going out there myself. As it is, we won't be able to send Cal any more help what with the storm and the FBI audit."

"Don't you mean today?"

"What?"

"The FBI is coming TODAY, Todd."

Dunn looked at his watch and groaned. "Shit. I've gotta go. Can you take care of our young friend there?"

"Consider it handled. Please let me know if there's anything I can do to assist with the investigation."

"You've already done more than you know, Doc. Thanks again."

Dunn left in a hurry. The first person he had to call was Cal. He'd love to know that their target was confirmed. Dunn placed the call as he rushed to the stairwell.

"Stokes."

"Cal, we just confirmed the kidnapper's identity."

"Is it who we thought?"

"Yes."

"Good, thanks."

"Hey, Cal?"

"Yeah."

"What's your next move?"

Dunn could hear the fierce determination in the Marine's voice. "I'm going to get Neil back."

CHAPTER 18

Cal gathered his men in the living room. Although most had just been awakened, he could feel the charged energy in the air. It was almost time to move. They waited expectantly for their young leader to speak.

"I just got confirmation from Dunn. The guy behind the kidnapping is a former soldier named Nick Ponder."

There were murmurs around the room. Apparently some of the men knew who Ponder was, and by the sound of the comments, their opinions were not favorable.

"According to Travis, this asshole is real piece of work. He's also downright deadly. Ponder has a habit of being connected with the wrong crowd. The two guys we brought in last night work for The Ponder Group. Unfortunately one of them got away, but that shouldn't matter."

Cal paused and looked around the room at his highly trained warriors. "Now, you know I'd never ask any one of you to do something that I wouldn't do myself...so I'll tell it to you straight. Once we find out where this Ponder guy lives, I'm going in there and taking him out. From what I've heard of the fucker, it probably should've been done a long time ago."

He searched his men for any sense of unease, but all he saw was seething anger. "So here's your chance. If you want out, tell me now. If you want in, pack your snow gear because we're headed into the mountains."

No one made a sound. The silence lingered until MSgt Trent spoke.

"Well, if Gaucho's going, I'm going."

"What are you talking about, Top?" asked Gaucho, confused about being called out.

"Hombre, I've been waitin' to see you freeze your cojones off for years!" The men snickered at the comment. Once again the large Marine succeeded in keeping the mood light. Cal loved him for it.

"Fuck you, Top," Gaucho replied with a grin.

Thirty minutes later they were putting the finishing touches on their plan. The biggest problem was figuring out what to do with their prisoner.

"Let's bring him along," suggested Brian.

Cal didn't like the idea. They'd have enough to worry about. Babysitting the overgrown child wasn't exactly what he had in mind.

"I'll take care of him, Cal." Everyone looked at Daniel in surprise. "I don't think he's a bad guy and I don't think he'll give us any trouble."

"I agree with Snake Eyes," offered Gaucho. "If we leave him here we'll have to leave two of our guys back too. Without any extra men coming from HQ, I think we need everybody we've got."

Cal wasn't sure. It wasn't that he didn't trust Daniel's judgment or skills. He knew the sniper could handle most men, but he would rather have the deadly warrior's eyes looking for coming threats.

"If you think you can handle it…okay. But you make sure he knows that if he slows us down even a bit, I'll tie his ass up and leave him on the mountain."

Daniel knew his boss wasn't that cruel, but he also knew Cal was deadly serious. He wouldn't stop until Neil was rescued. Daniel needed to have a good talk with Lance.

CHAPTER 19

Travis Haden walked into the conference room. Dunn, Haines and Dr. Higgins looked up from their discussion.

"I just got word from Cal. They're heading into the mountains soon." He walked over to the coffee pot to fill his mug.

"What are they doing with their prisoner?" asked Dunn.

"He's going along for the ride. Cal doesn't think the guy will give them any trouble."

"Do you really think that's a good idea?" asked Haines.

Travis shrugged. "It's Cal's operation, and I won't stand in his way. The good news is that by taking him the whole team will be together." Travis took a sip of his coffee. "Do we know when the FBI investigators are arriving?"

As the point person for the audit, Haines answered. "They should be here at seven."

Travis looked down at his watch. "That gives us just under two hours. I'm not worried about them finding anything with our contracts. Have we taken care of our little leak?"

"He's on his way to his very own private cell in the middle of nowhere, Skipper," responded Dunn. "Doc Higgins made a call and thirty minutes later a delivery van showed up at the gate and took the little shit out of here."

"Are we covered in case the Bureau asks questions about Mr. Zheng's whereabouts?"

"We've got the story all ironed out. He's taken a leave of absence due to mental instability," smirked Dunn, clearly not worried about the possibility of the story being dissected by the FBI.

"Good. Marge, who's running the show for the FBI?"

"A man named Jack Malone. I've checked with my contacts and he's got a good reputation within the Bureau. He's a thorough investigator but well-liked by his peers. Agent Malone's moved up the ladder swiftly over the last ten years. We're not the first security contractor he's audited. I don't think he'll be a problem."

Travis was still worried. Why had the FBI chosen this very moment to investigate SSI?

"Have they given you any indication as to why we're under the microscope?"

Haines shook her head. "Malone made it sound pretty routine. He even told me not to worry about it, that it's just our turn."

Something was wrong. Travis could feel it in his bones. "I want you to have their entire team monitored. Cell phones included."

Dunn looked at his boss cautiously. "You sure that's smart? What if they find out?"

"I'm not taking any chances right now, Todd. If they catch wind of it, tell them we monitor all non-SSI personnel.

If they really press it, have them talk to me. Something stinks about this whole thing, and I'll be damned if I let another rat into our house."

It was a risky move, but they all knew he was right. The sooner the FBI left the better.

CHAPTER 20

Cal's team loaded into the SUVs. They were taking enough cold weather gear and rations to last at least a week. Cal hoped they wouldn't have to test the duration.

The team would drive twenty minutes to the trailhead for Phelps Lake. To casual observers, the warriors would look like a group of hunters taking an extended trip into the Tetons. It wasn't one of the normal routes for gamesmen to take but not completely out of the ordinary.

Lance Upshaw was equally fitted with gear. Luckily, SSI's supply chief had sent some extra, just in case. Each man would carry a large mountaineering backpack with skis and snowshoes strapped to the outside. Due to the possibility of running into park rangers, they'd elected to bring along a mix of civilian hunting rifles and side arms. Each man also carried a collapsed H&K submachine gun in their packs. It wouldn't be the best thing if they were ambushed, but they'd have to make do.

Every man would be carrying around one hundred pounds on his back. It wouldn't be the easiest trek, but no one would complain. They'd all been through worse.

Twenty minutes later, the caravan pulled into the dirt parking lot at the trailhead. The sun was starting to peak out over the mountain range. It was the last sunlight they'd probably see for days. On Cal's last weather check it looked like the snowstorm would blow in around nine in the morning. It was imperative to make as much progress as possible before it hit.

The limited visibility would hamper their ability to travel and watch their flanks. It would've been a lot easier to take a helicopter, but every pilot they'd contacted had already grounded their aircraft because of the storm. Their only option was to hike in. It wouldn't be an easy journey, but they'd all endured far worse. Ponder's mountaintop headquarters was perfectly situated for its seclusion. Cal worried that the hideout was also an ideal stronghold.

They'd be humping up through the aptly named Death Canyon, then make their way toward Battleship Mountain. From the information headquarters had provided, it looked like Ponder's place was situated at the base of the northern side of Battleship Mountain.

It took five minutes for the men to strap on their packs, inspect their teammates and move out. Gaucho took point against Cal's request to be up front.

"We can do this without you, Boss. Let me get shot at first," the squat Hispanic said with a wink.

As they stepped off toward their destination, Cal could only hope that they wouldn't be too late.

———•———

At almost the same moment, the buyers' representatives were starting a similar journey from the west side of the mountain range. They'd prepped for the journey at the small Best Western in Driggs, Idaho the night before. None had slept. The small group of men was used to operating without sleep. Even their leader was a former commando and well-trained in cold weather warfare. Their country had fought for years in high altitudes. These men were the representatives sent by their homeland to deliver a new weapon that would transform their battle on a global front. Handpicked by their leader, each man was ready to die for their cause. Preparations had already been made in case they should perish.

The five operatives parked their two rented vehicles at the Teton Canyon Trail Head. Three minutes later they departed on foot toward Battleship Mountain.

———•———

Nick Ponder and Trapper were huddled over a topographic map of the area when the phone rang. Ponder answered with a grunt, listened, and then replaced the receiver.

"That was our buyers. They're on their way," Ponder muttered, deep in thought.

"You know when they'll be here?" asked Trapper.

Ponder shook his head. "They just said they're coming in on foot."

"I don't like it, Boss. It's bad enough that we've got the SSI guys headed our way. We don't have enough men to guard every pass leading into this place."

Ponder slammed his fist on the desk. "I know, goddamit! Just give me a minute to fucking think!"

Trapper held his tongue. He knew better than to press the point when his employer was upset. The man had a legendary temper, and Trapper wasn't in the mood to take a tongue lashing.

"How many men do we have?" Ponder asked for the fifth time.

Trapper stifled the urge to exhale before answering. "We've got twenty two, not including you and me. I figure we should keep at least half of them here at the complex. The rest we can break into two-man teams and post them on the most likely ingress routes."

The two men looked at the map again, and Ponder pointed to the positions he'd already selected in his mind.

"I want a team here, here and here. Make sure they'd got good radio equipment. I want to know as soon as they spot movement."

Over the years Ponder had secretly hoped for an invasion of his mountain lair. He'd prepared cave positions in strategic locations to serve as forward outposts. Ponder had played the scenario over and over again in his dreams. He was pretty sure some of his ancestors had died defending castles from invading armies. It was in his blood.

Ponder was sure that his small army could hold off anything but a full-scale assault by an overwhelming force. Even now his men were mounting heavy machine guns and other defensive weapons around the perimeter of his compound.

Tucked into the side of Battleship Mountain, Ponder's headquarters was a perfectly designed fortress. It was well concealed and afforded a perfect view of the large mountain basin to the northeast. The only way to assault the stronghold was from the basin. It was possible to skirt the ledge that ran from northwest to southeast, but it would also be suicidal considering the perfect field of fire possessed by the defenders. Ponder at one point thought it was possible for an invading force to come over Battlefield Mountain and walk down the mountain. That was until two winters before when he'd tried it himself. He'd almost died trying to traverse the steep slope. Knowing that, Ponder had designed a beautiful kill zone right in his front yard. The SSI assault team wouldn't have a chance.

"I want you here with me coordinating everything."

Trapper made a face at his boss's order.

"What is it?" Ponder growled.

"I was kinda hoping you'd let me go find the SSI guys."

"By yourself?" Ponder asked incredulously.

Trapper smiled. "This ain't my first rodeo, Boss."

Ponder knew the man was right. They called him Trapper for a reason. He had a talent for finding and getting rid of people no matter the time or place.

"So you know where they're coming from?"

Trapper nodded with a sly grin.

"Are you gonna tell me?" Ponder solicited.

"Let me make sure, and I'll call it in as soon as I've got eyes-on."

Although Ponder trusted his Lieutenant, his gut was telling him to order Trapper to stay at the compound. He shook the thought off as quickly as it had come. He'd be a lot better off if one man could decimate the SSI band.

"Fine, but make sure you take care of deploying our men before you go."

They finalized their campaign and toasted their victory over a welcomed shot of Jack Daniels.

CHAPTER 21

CAMP SPARTAN
ARRINGTON, TN
7:00AM CST, SEPTEMBER 28TH

The FBI contingent arrived precisely at 7:00am. Four black Chevy Suburbans rolled through Camp Spartan's front gate and headed to the SSI's headquarters.

Travis, Todd and Marge met the investigators in the entryway. An average-looking man in his early forties led the way. His thinning hair and deep bags under his eyes belied his stressful position. He walked right up to Travis and offered his hand.

"Mr. Haden, I'm Jack Malone. Thanks for meeting us."

"Please, call me Travis."

Introductions were made and the group made its way to the large conference room reserved for the occasion. There was coffee and a mixed assortment of breakfast food arranged for their guests.

"Thanks for the food and coffee, Marge," Malone offered. "We don't always get the best reception during our audits."

Haines gave the agent a thin smile. "There's no reason for us not to be cordial. We know that this is just one of the requirements of being in the security business."

Malone smiled and grabbed a glazed donut. "I hope you don't mind if I grab a bite while we talk. I didn't get a chance to eat anything earlier. I'm starving."

He quickly devoured three donuts and washed it down with some coffee. The others took seats around the conference table as they ate.

Still standing, Malone wiped his mouth and addressed the SSI leadership. "Like I told Ms. Haines over the phone, we're here to do a routine audit. Somehow you've avoided the list all these years." He smiled at his joke. "We'll try to make it as painless as possible. Starting with your accounting department, my crew will dig into your operations over the past five to ten years. As long as there aren't any discrepancies, we'll be out of your hair in a day and a half, two tops."

Travis wasn't worried about the FBI uncovering their covert division. There were no files. All their equipment was purchased with cash or handled through one of the many offshore accounts administered by Neil Patel. Haden's only concern was not being able to actively monitor Cal's team out west. Cal was on his own.

"Just let us know what you need to look at and we'll get it to you. I'll be in my office if you need me," Travis said.

"Thanks. Okay then. Let's head over to accounting."

Travis pulled Marge aside as the rest of the entourage filed out of the room.

"Let me know if you hear anything. I'm about to put in a call to one of our friends in D.C."

"Who?"

"Zimmer."

Congressman Brandon Zimmer was a first term representative from Massachusetts. He'd recently been involved in a nasty encounter with a group of Japanese imperialists looking to relive Japan's glory days. Cal's team had helped Zimmer uncover the plot by Zimmer's now deceased father, Senator Richard Zimmer, to claim the Presidency. The younger Zimmer had proved his worth by eliminating his father before the President could be killed. Brandon was now part of a very secretive group of retired politicians known as the Council of Patriots. Only a handful of people in the world knew of the Council's existence.

"Are you sure that's a good idea? Isn't he in the middle of the special election for his father's Senate seat?"

"Marge, you know he owes us big time. Besides, I just want him to see if he can pull some strings and find out why we're being investigated. I don't believe this bullshit about a routine audit."

They agreed to meet again at lunch to discuss any developments. Travis walked to his office and placed the call.

CHAPTER 22

Brandon Zimmer was enjoying a much-needed morning off from campaigning. The last week had been a whirlwind of hand-shaking, speeches and phone calls. Washington insiders believed that the young Congressman would likely win an overwhelming victory against his opponent. It hadn't hurt that former President Hank Waller made the unexpected move of publicly endorsing Zimmer for the vacated seat. Preliminary polls were showing Brandon with almost seventy-five percent of the likely vote.

He'd learned from experience not to take a lead for granted and pushed his campaign staff hard. Zimmer was in the middle of perusing the college football matchups for the coming weekend when his cell phone rang. He looked at the caller ID and smiled.

"Hey, Trav!"

"Good morning, Congressman…or should I be calling you Senator now?"

"Not yet, and you know you can always call me Brandon."

"I know." Travis paused.

Brandon caught the hesitation. "What's going on?"

"Are you on the cell phone we gave you?"

"Yeah. Why?" Zimmer perked up at the question. Travis typically got right to the point.

Travis quickly outlined the details of Neil's kidnapping and Cal's operation to get him back.

"God, I'm sorry. Do you think he's still alive?"

"To be honest with you, I'm not sure. Then again, I don't know why this guy would go through all the trouble to take Neil just to kill him."

"Do you have a motive?"

"Not yet, but I'm sure we'll find out soon enough."

"How can I help?" Zimmer asked.

"Actually, I called to ask for your help with something else," Travis answered cryptically.

Now Brandon was really confused. "Something else?"

"Yeah. It just so happens that as soon as we got Cal to Wyoming, the FBI says it's time for an audit. They just got here."

Travis didn't have to tell Zimmer that the timing was more than a little coincidental. "So you think it has something to do with what's going on with Neil?"

"I do. If my hands weren't tied with our guests, I'd make some phone calls. I was wondering if you wouldn't mind making some discrete inquiries within your little club."

Brandon knew he was talking about the Council of Patriots. The combined Rolodex of the two former Presidents and the seven former senators and congressmen in the group made for a powerful information-gathering asset. It was, however, important not to drink from the well too often. The Council's secrecy was paramount.

"Let me call our friends and see how they can help."

"I really appreciate it, Brandon. Please call me if you find out anything."

"I will. And, Trav…?"

"Yeah?"

"Call me for help any time."

"Roger."

Zimmer ended the call and sat for a moment. He had a lot of pressing matters to attend to this afternoon, but this would take priority. He owed Cal and Neil a huge debt. If it weren't for them, he'd probably be in jail and the President would be dead. Brandon would do anything to help his new friends.

He picked up his cell phone again and scrolled through his contact list. After pressing the right record, he held the phone to his ear. The call connected and Zimmer spoke. "Mr. President, I need a moment of your time."

CHAPTER 23

"Rise and shine!" Ponder's bellow was followed by a kick to Neil's wobbly cot. Neil just barely caught himself before he fell off and onto the floor.

He looked up at his captor through bleary eyes. He'd just managed to fall asleep and suspected Ponder had waited for his slumber just to torment him.

"What time is it?" Neil dared to ask.

"I said it's time to rise and shine! Now get cleaned up. We're taking you back to the server room." Ponder stormed out of the cell.

It was the same journey they'd repeatedly forced him to make. He'd resisted their requests but knew his time was running short. Neil had to deliver something or else they'd kill him.

He sat up painfully. Shivering uncontrollably, Neil wrapped the thin blanket around his shrinking body. Although his time in captivity hadn't been long, Neil knew he'd already lost weight. The constant stress led to a complete lack of appetite in the normally fit Indian-American. Somehow he managed to force down several bites of food every time the jailer brought it. He knew it wasn't enough.

Just as he'd fallen asleep, the tech genius was trying to think of a way to alert his friends at SSI. If he had more time with a computer it would've been easy, but every time they set him at the workstation there was someone watching.

The guard arrived and unceremoniously picked Neil up like a baby and carried him out of the cell. A minute later they arrived at the now familiar server room. It wasn't much compared to what Neil was used to, but still impressive for a mountain top retreat.

Ponder stood over his shoulder just as he had done before. "Let's try this again. Are you going to do it or not?"

Neil didn't have the will to say no. What reserves he'd had now lay scattered on the frozen ground outside the complex. "I'll do it."

Ponder was secretly relieved. "Now remember what I told you," Ponder growled as he extracted a large knife from its leg holster, "you try anything funny and I'll take off your other foot personally."

Neil didn't doubt the man's threat. In the short time he'd been a guest at Chateau Winter Wonderland, as Neil now thought of the compound, he'd come to realize that the man in charge was not only ruthless, but probably had a few screws loose upstairs. His ability to pivot from anger to mirth spoke volumes of the grizzled man's mental faculties.

Shifting uncomfortably, Neil moved closer to the computer's keypad. He tried to place his hand on the mouse but his hands kept shaking.

Ponder turned to his sentry and barked, "Get a couple space heaters over here and bring some more blankets too. Have the cook bring down some hot soup and cider."

He looked down at Neil. "Well what are you waiting for? Get back to work!"

Neil whipped his head back around and did his best to grip the mouse and click through the screens.

———◆———

Trapper was making good time on the mule he'd saddled. Something told him that the SSI operators would take the Death Canyon entrance. It was well traveled and easy to access from Teton Village. Trapper had already confirmed with the few helicopter companies in the area that no one had booked a flight. That left his enemy with only one option: trek in on foot.

He pushed his mule hard hoping he'd make his destination before the storm hit. If he did, the slaughter would be easy. He'd have a perfect view. The former soldier grinned as he imagined the coming battle.

———◆———

The men were silent as they moved swiftly down the trail. They'd made good time so far and hadn't encountered many hikers. The few people they had seen were going the opposite way, eager to avoid the blizzard. Everyone could feel the weather shift as the storm crept closer. Cal was hiking in the middle of pack, allowing his mind to drift back to his days in the Marine Corps, hiking countless miles with fellow Marines.

Brian Ramirez pulled up beside him.

"What's going on, Doc? Not enough action in the rear?"

Brian had elected to stay in the back of the group just as he'd done during his time with Marines. It was customary for the Corpsman to tend to the stragglers and injured with the company gunny.

"Was wondering if you'd heard anything else from Camp Spartan."

Cal shook his head. "They're busy handling the FBI guys that someone shoved down their throats. I can't believe I'm saying this, but I'd rather be here than dealing with that right now."

Brian agreed. "So we're really going in as is? No more support from home?"

"It's just us, Doc."

Brian wasn't the only one that couldn't shake the feeling that they were walking into a shitstorm.

"I know what you're thinking, Doc, but our options are limited. We know where they're keeping Neil so we've gotta go get him."

"But how do we know for sure that he's up there?"

Cal was getting tired of the conversation. Brian was one of his best friends, but the last thing he needed right now was to have his judgment questioned.

"It's all we've got to go on. Look, I gave everyone the chance to stay back. If you think it's such a bad idea feel free to turn around now," Cal noticed a couple of the men around them glance back in concern.

"You know I wouldn't do that, Cal. I just want to make sure you've thought this whole thing through. I'm not trying to make waves. I just want to help."

Cal calmed in response to Brian's conciliatory tone. The stress was getting to him. He knew he had to be careful and keep his temper in check. Nothing good came of barking at his team.

"Sorry, Doc. Just forget what I said. I couldn't do this without you."

"Don't worry about it. Is there anything I can do to help?"

"Just make sure you catch Top when he falls out back there," Cal said loudly enough for the huge Marine Master Sergeant to hear.

"I heard that!" Trent boomed as loudly as he dared.

The men around them chuckled quietly.

"Seriously though, Doc, we just need to get up there as soon as we can. I'm afraid of what they're planning for Neil."

"Yeah," Brian said absently.

It was good that they had the winding path to worry about because it was impossible to imagine the fate of their friend. By now they'd all heard the stories about Nick Ponder's exploits. There wasn't a man in the group that didn't want to see the man in jail or dead.

Brian dropped back to the rear of the formation and left Cal to his thoughts.

CHAPTER 24

"Okay, I'm in," announced Neil.

Ponder strained to make sense of the code on the monitor. A second later the screen changed and displayed the control panel of the Shiloh Wind Power Plant in Bird's Landing, California.

"Shut it down," Ponder ordered.

He'd told Neil on their first attempt that the test was to shut down the plant's power for a full minute. Neil knew it would be an easy feat with his computer prowess. Hell, with his own equipment he'd have done it in less than five minutes. In Ponder's lair he'd had to build a hacking system from scratch. Although labor intensive, it had allowed Patel to imbed some extra code into the program. He hoped it would be enough to alert his friends of his location.

"I said shut it down!"

Neil did as he was told.

Miles away at the Shiloh Wind Power Plant, Bernice Ormand was monitoring the plant's computer systems. She'd been in the control room since 6:00am and casually swept her gaze across the assorted meters. Bernice still marveled at the newly computerized system. She'd been at the power plant since it opened in 2006. Back then they'd installed a very rudimentary monitoring system just to get the plant built under budget. It wasn't until the new President was elected in 2008, and his green energy funding went into effect, that the Shiloh Wind Power Plant installed a completely computer driven monitoring system.

Bernice sipped her second green tea of the morning as she jotted down some notes in the plant's logbook. As she went to complete her entry, all the screens on the panel went dark.

"What in the world?" Bernice said.

She grabbed the phone and dialed the station manager.

"Stan, it's Bernice. The monitoring system just went down."

"I'm checking one of the turbines right now. I'll be up in five minutes."

Stan seemed unconcerned and his attitude served to calm Bernice's nerves. She'd never seen this happen before. They'd had intermittent issues with malfunctioning turbines in the past, but the monitoring systems had always performed flaw-lessly. By the time she'd collected her thoughts enough to grab the logbook the computer screens flickered back to life.

Huh. I better call Stan back, she thought. Bernice picked up the phone and dialed the manager's number again.

"The computers are back online, Stan."

"Good. Let me know if it happens again. Thanks, Bernice."

She hung up the phone, entered the incident into the logbook, then grabbed her Sudoku puzzle book and dove into her unfinished brainteaser.

"The system is back online," Neil declared somberly.

"Well I'll be damned!" Ponder exulted. "Get him back to his cell so I can make a phone call," he told his employee.

As the jailer took Patel back to his room, Ponder pulled out his cell phone and dialed his contact's number.

"Yeah, it's me. Are you happy now?" Ponder asked.

"We have received confirmation of the test results. One half of the purchase price will be deposited into escrow. I will email you the deposit receipt momentarily." The line went dead.

Ponder almost drooled at the thought. He was so close to wrapping up the deal. Now he could focus on tying up some loose ends. With barely concealed glee he placed another call.

"Are you there yet?" he asked his right hand man.

"Almost," Trapper said breathlessly. Ponder could hear the man being jostled as he rode.

"Good. We just passed our test so the buy is a go."

"Congrats, Boss. How about I take care of our friends and then you buy the first round in Bora Bora?"

"You got it," Ponder responded, almost cheerfully.

He replaced the phone in his pocket and allowed himself a second to take in the moment. In a matter of hours he would be a very rich man.

The buyer's agent answered the silent ringing.

"Yes?"

"You have authorization to proceed."

"Understood." The man ended the call and scanned the surrounding area. His men were ready for a fight. They moved silently through the mountainous terrain, ever vigilant through years of hard training. He wondered if the seller even suspected what would soon happen. Doubtful. The arrogant Americans never suspected treachery when a payday was close at hand. They were greedy and short-sighted. It was all the more reason to crush them. The foreign emissary relished the thought and plodded along with his assassins.

CHAPTER 25

True to Jack Malone's word, the investigation progressed swiftly. SSI employees were accommodating and the FBI agents were courteous in their questioning. Marjorie Haines was hopeful that it would all end soon. She had more important things to do than monitor their visitors.

Her phone rang and she answered. "Haines."

"Marge, it's Dunn. I've got something you need to see right now."

"Where are you?"

"In the Batcave."

Haines looked at her watch then over at the FBI teams going through paperwork. Jack Malone had left earlier to take a tour of the campus.

"Give me a minute to excuse myself and I'll be right down, Todd."

Marge checked to make sure that the investigators didn't need her for a few minutes, and then headed to meet up with SSI security chief.

———————

Dunn was staring at a computer screen when Marge entered the Batcave. He had two of Neil's computer techs assisting. They were watching a video. As she got closer, she realized the recording was of Agent Malone.

"What's going on, Todd?"

Dunn turned around, surprised by the interruption. "Oh hey, that was fast."

"It sounded important so I got over here as quickly as I could."

"It is. Come take a look."

The two techs made room as Haines squeezed in to get a better view.

"Tell me what I'm looking at."

The tech with a head full of unruly red hair spoke up first. "Well, Ms. Haines, Mr. Dunn told us to keep tabs on all the FBI guys. It was pretty easy until this guy…"

"Agent Malone," Haines furnished.

"Yeah, until Agent Malone went on a tour of the campus with Kendall from operations."

Haines was confused. "What do you mean *until*?"

The tech scratched his scraggly beard, unfazed by Marge's tone. "Well, as long as he was in one of our buildings it was easy to jump from one camera to the next and follow him. It was when he went outside that we had a problem."

"How so?" Haines asked impatiently.

"We have a limited number of cameras in the outdoor areas. They're mostly at the front gate and around the perimeter. There's usually no need to have them. So that posed a slight problem. How could we watch and listen in on what he was doing?"

"I'm sorry…"

"Bowser."

"Your name is Bowser?"

"Actually my name's Patrick but everybody calls me Bowser."

"Okay, Bowser, tell me what you did to fix the problem."

"You know that Neil built his Baby Birds a while back…"

Baby Bird was the nickname the SSI operators had given to Neil's tiny surveillance drone. The thing looked like a helicopter, fit in the palm of your hand and could be controlled hands-free with a special pair of sunglasses similar to the eye control systems used by Apache pilots.

"…and we've outfitted a couple of them with long range microphones. We launched two of them to follow Agent Malone while he was outside."

"Bowser, this is all very fascinating, but would you please mind getting to the point?" Haines requested as politely as she could muster.

"Sorry, Ms. Haines. Anyway, long story short, once they got near the chow hall Agent Malone asks if he can use one of the Porta-Johns the construction crews are using. He said he had too much coffee and really had to take a leak."

Haines rolled her eyes and motioned for the young tech to hurry up with his explanation.

"So he walks over to the Porta-John and, once he's out of earshot from Kendall, he pulls out his cell phone."

Dunn interrupted, "So that's where we'll start the video for you."

Bowser took the cue and started the video. It showed Agent Malone walking to the blue porta-potty. He paused just as someone would do if their phone rang in their pocket. Malone extracted his cell phone, pressed a button, then held it to his ear.

"Hey, I'm in." The recording was scratchy, but Haines could make out every word.

Malone listened to the person on the other end of the call.

"Yeah. After I take this little tour and let them soften up a bit I'll ask for your little buddy Zheng. Once I get my hands on him, I'll order him to start opening up all the locked doors in this place."

He listened again and nodded.

"Don't worry, I'll get him out of here, but it's gonna cost you extra."

Malone paused to listen and then chuckled. "Sure, I'm ready for a little vacation too. Let's wrap this up and then I'll use some of my accrued leave. At least the Bureau gives me that much. I'll call you in a couple hours."

Haines's normally calm face raged red. "Do we know who he talked to?"

"Bowser tracked it to a tower in the Jackson Hole area," Dunn answered, dead serious. "You want me to take care of this?"

Haines thought for a moment. What they should do is turn the piece-of-shit-Malone in to his superiors. But Haines came from a warrior background. Her father was a former Special Forces soldier who'd fought in Vietnam. She probably would have tried to become an infantry officer if the military allowed it.

"I'll take care of Agent Malone. Bowser, can you email that video to me?" Bowser nodded. "Todd, would you mind setting up one of your interrogation rooms?"

The two techs looked at Haines in awe. They'd heard rumors of her physical prowess, and she was undoubtedly beautiful, but seeing the lioness come out right before their eyes was astonishing.

Dunn and Haines went to leave, but Bowser had one more question.

"Hey, Ms. Haines, what's Z...uh, I mean what's Terrence Zheng got to do with all this?"

Haines stopped and turned around. "Loose lips sink ships, gentlemen. You won't be seeing Mr. Zheng any time soon."

Without another word, she turned away and left the room, Dunn in tow.

Bowser looked at his companion in wide-eyed wonder. "I call dibs on Zheng's Xbox profile!"

◆

Dunn split off as Haines walked swiftly to the security desk. "Can you please ask Agent Malone to join me in the lower level observation deck?" she asked the large sentry.

"Yes, Ms. Haines. I'll escort him down personally."

"Thank you."

Haines headed back toward the Batcave. As an afterthought, she pulled out her phone as she walked.

"Travis, I think we've found the connection."

Fifteen minutes later, Malone, escorted by the guard, entered the gallery overlooking the interrogation rooms. With a nod from Dunn, the guard left and Malone joined him and Haines.

"So what's up?" Malone asked conspiratorially. "Is this where you do your secret interrogations?"

Haines answered with a dry laugh. "I just thought you might like to see this and get a quick tour. It's state of the art and where we do all our training for new SSI personnel going into the field."

"Nice," Malone admired as he gazed down at the brightly lit rooms. "Lead on, Ms. Haines!"

Dunn made no move to follow. "You're not coming with us, Dunn?" Agent Malone asked.

"I've got some things to take care of upstairs. We'll have lunch waiting for you when you're finished here." Dunn headed to the stairwell and disappeared.

Haines led Malone to the control room first. He gave it a cursory examination and, once satisfied, indicated they should move on to the lower rooms.

They stepped down the side staircase and entered the first room they encountered.

"As you can see, we have cameras installed there and there," Haines pointed to the locations of the observation equipment. "And anyone in the gallery can watch through the one-way window."

Agent Malone traced his hand along the edge of the metal table in the center of the room. He stared at Haines lasciviously. "You want to tell me why you really wanted to get me down here…alone?"

"I don't know what you're talking about, Jack," Haines answered in feigned surprise.

"You could've gotten anyone to show me this place. Why did you want to bring me down here?"

Haines looked back at Malone with an embarrassed shrug. "Am I that obvious?" she asked innocently.

Agent Malone's eyes lit up as he moved closer to the attractive attorney. "Well, I can't say that I'm surprised."

"Oh?"

"You're surrounded by these meatheads all day long. I'm not surprised you're more attracted to the polished type."

"And you're saying you're the polished type?" Haines purred.

"I am."

"So what should we do now?"

Malone glanced up to the invisible cameras. "What about witnesses?" he asked.

"I turned those off when we were in the control room."

"And what about someone seeing us from the gallery?"

Haines smiled mischievously. "I told Dunn to give us some time alone. We should have plenty of time." She slinked up to Malone and placed a hand on his chest. Suddenly, he seemed nervous and uncertain.

"Would you feel more comfortable if I turned off the lights?" Haines asked.

Malone could only nod through parched lips and slowed brain function. *Is this really happening?*

Haines walked to the door and turned off the lights. The room was thrust into darkness except for the small amount of light seeping in through the one-way mirror.

"Where are you, Jack?"

"Over here," Malone responded hoarsely. He started to loosen his tie so he could breathe.

Seconds later, Haines's hands were back on his chest and he could feel her hot breath on his neck.

"So how do you want to do this?" he asked.

"I thought we'd get to know each other a little bit first," she teased, yanking down playfully on his tie.

"Uh, sure. What would you like to know?"

"Oh, I just have one question for you, Jack." She grazed her nose along his jaw line, and he shuddered in anticipation.

"Okay. What's your question, Ms. Haines?"

She took his head in her hands and brought his ear down to her mouth. "I just want to know one thing. How long did it take before you turned traitor?"

Before Malone had time to respond, Haines blasted her knee into his groin. As he doubled over in pain, she bent down and whispered in his ear one last time. "Now you know why they call me The Hammer, you piece of shit."

Grabbing his head again, she slammed her knee into his temple and let him drop unconscious onto the floor. Marge checked to see that he had a pulse, then grabbed the hand-cuffs from Malone's belt and strapped his two hands behind his back. After relieving the crooked agent of his sidearm, Haines left the room to fetch Dr. Higgins.

Agent Jack Malone kicked and screamed as Dr. Higgins wheeled in his tools. The guards had strapped him to a gurney as he lay unconscious.

"I don't know what that bitch told you, but you guys are in some deep shit. I am an FBI agent!"

Higgins ignored the man and continued to set up his supplies.

"Talk to me!" yelled Malone.

The expert interrogator continued to pay him no heed. Higgins liked to get a first impression of his subjects. It allowed him to assess the person's demeanor in order to administer the correct dosage of his truth serum. Agent Malone might be a challenge, but the wizened doctor relished the test.

Higgins finally turned to face Malone. "Mr. Malone, I am here to ask you some very specific questions. I will tell you that it's pointless trying to resist. Either tell me the truth or we'll extract it in other ways."

Malone's eyes bulged in anger. "You fucking quack! I'm gonna have your ass for this! You know how illegal…!"

Instead of listening further, Dr. Higgins adjusted the mechanical gurney to give him better access to the apparatus. Malone silenced as soon as he saw the needles. "What… what's that for?"

"I told you, Mr. Malone, if you don't want to cooperate, we'll coax you into cooperating."

"What are you talking about? I'm here to investigate YOU!"

"I guess you could say the shoe is on the other foot now, wouldn't you?" Higgins asked.

Malone kept screaming obscenities until Dr. Higgins inserted the IV needle into his arm. Higgins waited five minutes for the drug to fully take hold. He could see that Malone was completely relaxed.

"There, now that's better. How are you feeling, Mr. Malone?"

"I'm…nice." Malone's face was calm. It looked like the drug had performed as planned.

"Is it okay if I ask you some questions now, Mr. Malone?"

"Sure," answered the suspect dreamily.

Like Zheng before, Agent Malone was more than happy to answer any and all questions. Malone described his relationship with Nick Ponder. They'd met while serving in the Army and reconnected six years earlier when Agent Malone had been part of the team that audited The Ponder Group. They shared a love of fast women and money. Over the years, Malone had come to Ponder's rescue, for a price. Files were misplaced and agents were reassigned from ongoing investigations. Malone knew how to manipulate people and the system. They'd both become wealthy through the mutually beneficial relationship.

"How is it that you came to investigate SSI?" Higgins asked, knowing that Dunn and Haines were digesting every word in the control room.

"I got a call from Nick. He said he needed SSI out of his hair for a while. Told me it would be helpful if we could run a little investigation. Nick said he had a guy on the inside that was feeding him intel and that there might just be some juicy stuff in it for me."

"So you were tasked with keeping us busy?"

"Yeah, but the silver lining for me was finding something that could shut down your whole operation."

"Did Mr. Ponder give you any specifics on what you might find?"

"Not really, but this Zheng kid was supposed to start the digging. Hey, where is Zheng anyway?"

"Mr. Zheng is no longer your concern, Mr. Malone."

Malone shrugged nonchalantly.

Higgins had all the information they would need. A condensed version of the recording would be delivered to one of their contacts in the Hoover Building. Jack Malone would be quietly put away in a maximum-security federal prison. The FBI didn't like traitors and dealt with them swiftly.

"It was a pleasure speaking with you, Mr. Malone. Best of luck in the future."

Higgins gathered his gear and headed for the door.

———

Dr. Higgins joined Marge Haines and Todd Dunn in the gallery.

"I've gotta say, Doc, you are an artist when it comes to making people talk," Dunn offered, impressed yet again by the doctor's skill.

"Lots and lots of practice, Todd. Although I must say that with a man like Mr. Malone, sometimes I wish I could deliver some damage like Marjorie."

It was hard to get Haines to blush and yet she did. She held Dr. Higgins in high esteem and sought his insight often. "I'll start giving you classes in the gym whenever you're ready, Doctor."

Higgins chuckled warmly. "That's quite all right. I'll leave the tough stuff to you and the boys."

"On to a more serious topic," Dunn interrupted, "I've already emailed the edited transcript to a buddy of mine at the Bureau. I'm thinking this audit will be over before we know it."

Haines and Higgins nodded. Once the FBI found out that one of their investigative teams had been tasked under false pretences, they would likely do everything they could to extract their people as soon as possible.

"Is there anything else you'd like me to do?" Dr. Higgins asked his colleagues.

Dunn shook his head. "As long as we don't have any other traitors in our midst, I think we're good."

"Any word from Cal?"

"The last we heard they were a couple hours into their insertion." Dunn looked at his watch. "They should be getting a good dose of the storm right about now."

CHAPTER 26

As soon as the storm hit, they couldn't see five feet in front of them. Although it definitely slowed their forward progress, it also gave them cover should anyone be tracking from a higher elevation.

Cal's team had donned all white coveralls as the snow started to fall. The white camouflage would further conceal them from enemy eyes.

They were still walking through the middle of Death Canyon, but wouldn't for much longer. It had been a gamble to take the well used path in order to speed their progress. Cal glanced at his GPS. They were nearing their scheduled checkpoint. After a short rest, the group would break into two teams. They'd approach the objective from two directions.

Cal and Daniel would accompany Gaucho. Lance Upshaw, the helpful prisoner, would also be with Cal's group.

MSgt Trent and Brian Ramirez would go with the other team.

The halt signal was passed back through the dispersed formation. Cal made his way to the front. Gaucho was rooting through a pack of cold weather rations as Cal moved up next to him.

"How are you liking the weather, Gaucho?"

The Hispanic warrior made a comical face. With the snow already starting to stick to his braided bearded, Cal thought his team leader was starting to look more and more like a mountain dwarf from the *Lord of the Rings*.

"I'm gonna freeze my nuts off tonight!"

Cal laughed. "That's only if we stop moving. How much longer do you think we have?"

Gaucho pulled out his map and pointed to their current location. "As long as we keep making good time I think we'll get there just after midnight."

Cal looked up at the obscured sky. The snowfall was picking up and already starting to accumulate. He guessed that there was already a good three inches on the ground.

"I'll tell you that I'm not looking forward to putting these damn skis on, Boss." Gaucho looked back at the cross-country skis strapped to his pack.

Cal could only image what the short Mexican would look like on skis.

"At least we'll have skins for when we're going uphill. You ever tried to go up a slope without them?"

Gaucho nodded sadly. "I think the Army played a trick on me when they sent me to your Marine Mountain Warfare Training Center in Bridgeport."

Cal snorted at the thought. He'd spent six weeks at the remote training center with his battalion as a young corporal. Fully half of the Marines in his unit ended up not finishing the training mostly from injury or illness. Some just couldn't take the altitude and the cold. He remembered being in shock when some of the toughest Marines in his company had refused to go back up the mountain. Cold weather separated the men from the boys even amongst Marines.

"That big kid giving Snake Eyes any trouble?" Gaucho asked.

"He's kept pretty quiet. Hasn't complained once. Daniel even said he offered to carry more gear before we stepped off."

"No shit?"

Cal nodded. "I think he's getting it through his head that we're not the bad guys. He might even come in handy when we get close to Ponder's place."

⸺•⸺

Lance Upshaw had come to the realization that he'd probably been playing for the wrong team since joining The Ponder Group. There'd been warning signs, like when a couple of new guys had disappeared on an overseas op. Ponder had merely shrugged and noted that it was the price of doing business in a dangerous world. There were no memorials and no letters of condolence.

Then there were the actual men that Ponder hired. Most had washed out of the military for one reason or another. At first Lance thought it was a blessing that a man like Nick Ponder would lend a helping hand to men who needed a second chance. It didn't take Lance long to see that most of Ponder's contractors didn't deserve a second chance. They were bullies and criminals. In his third month of employment, Lance had to fight off three separate challengers until the rest had realized that he was more than a match for them. Now they mostly left him alone.

And that's how he'd felt for most of the past year. Luckily Trapper had recognized Lance's work ethic and took him along when he needed some muscle. It wasn't bad work but Lance still felt unsatisfied. There had to be more to life.

Since being captured by the SSI guys, he'd quietly observed their interactions. It was obvious they all respected one another. Also, despite the fact that he was the enemy, they still treated him with respect. Not once had any of the men degraded him, and it all started with Daniel Briggs. In Briggs, Lance saw the Marine he wished he himself had become. Silent in his approach, the man the others called Snake Eyes was obviously a highly valued part of the team. And he did it all without yelling or cussing. In fact, Lance could have sworn that he'd once seen Briggs say a prayer and then finish with the sign of the cross.

It all gave the disgraced Marine a lot to think about. These men were walking into almost certain danger, all for the love of a friend. *Would Nick Ponder do the same thing?* Lance didn't think so.

⎯⎯⎯◆⎯⎯⎯

Far above, Trapper rubbed his hands to ward off the cold. Although he couldn't see the troops moving into his territory, he had laid small pressure plates along the trail to alert him of their passing. He silently congratulated himself for choosing the right route. Now all he needed to do was track and take them out once the time was right.

CHAPTER 27

Ponder paced back and forth on the hardwood floor. The pieces were coming together, but he still had some concerns. Most importantly, he hadn't heard from either Terrence Zheng or Jack Malone. His greedy mind hoped they were too busy to call because they were torpedoing SSI.

Ponder figured that it was impossible for a security contractor not to be into some kind of illegal activity. Hell, he'd skirted the law for years. Jack Malone knew how to find things and would be even more effective with the Zheng's help.

Still, he couldn't shake the thought that something was wrong. He moved to his laptop and checked the email account he shared with Zheng. Nothing. Next he scrolled through his other email accounts for word from Jack. Nothing again.

Ponder allowed himself to think about the worst case scenario. If the assholes at SSI had figured out not only his involvement, but also the actions of Zheng and Malone, his path was less certain. The thing he had to focus on was the

144

money that would soon be in his bank accounts. He'd scatter the funds to the four corners of the globe through transfers he'd already arranged with his international brokers. Ponder would be paying some hefty fees, but it would be worth it. With his money safely stashed he could make a new home anywhere.

Cracking his knuckles, he imagined Trapper silently stalking his quarry. If he survived, fine. If not, there would be one less person to pay from his treasure chest. Ponder smiled despite his nerves. Maybe a new house in Costa Rica was just what he needed.

CHAPTER 28

"Are they all gone?" Travis asked Dunn, who'd just stepped into his office.

"Yeah. The last SUV just rolled out with Agent Jack Malone hog-tied in the back."

"Did you get everything squared away with the Bureau?"

Dunn nodded. "We shouldn't have another audit for a while. They even apologized and thanked me for helping with Malone."

"Good. Let's get some more personnel out to Cal."

"Isn't the weather turning to shit out there, Skipper?"

Travis's eyes went cold. "I don't care. If they can't fly onto that fucking mountain, get them as close as we can."

"I'll go with them and make sure it's done."

"I can't spare you right now, Todd. We've got to…"

"I'm going, Skipper," Dunn interrupted curtly.

Travis looked at his friend in surprise. He couldn't remember the last time Dunn had put his foot down. The fact was he'd gotten used to having Dunn around. With his own time in the field effectively at an end, he'd kept his head of security with him. Although barely in their forties, but still fit enough to be in any Special Forces unit, they'd both become consumed with the day-to-day running of SSI. There were times Travis longed to be on the battlefield again. His position as CEO pretty much negated that option.

"I guess it would be wasted breath trying to persuade you to stay?"

"It would."

"Why now?"

"Honestly?"

"Honestly," Travis answered.

"Two reasons. First, it's been a while since I've been out with the boys. No disrespect, Skipper, but sticking close to the office can wear on a guy."

Travis smiled and motioned for Dunn to go on.

"Second, I've got a really bad feeling on this one. I think Cal's gonna need every man he can get."

"Then let's get our things packed," suggested Travis, already heading to the locker room.

"Wait…but you can't go!"

Travis swiveled around and flashed Dunn a sly grin. "Why not? I'm the boss. I think you're right. Cal needs every man we can spare."

Dunn's mouth was hanging open. He couldn't order his boss to stay behind.

"But what about…?"

Travis stopped the question with a raised hand. "Come on, Todd. If things blow up in our face it's not gonna be because I jumped on a plane to rescue my cousin."

Dunn knew he was right. They were both warriors and felt compelled to run to the sound of battle.

"Okay. You let Haines know what we're doing - she's gonna shit by the way - and I'll mobilize the men and book the flight."

"Make sure you get the craziest SOB pilot you can find. We'll need one to fly into that snowstorm."

Dunn returned his boss's smile and said, "I think I know just where to find one."

———

Thirty minutes later, Travis, Dunn and twenty four fully loaded SSI warriors climbed into three separate helicopters. They'd make the quick hop to Nashville International Airport and then catch a special flight out to Wyoming.

Travis put on a headset so he could talk to Dunn.

"Who are we meeting at the airport?"

Dunn smirked at the question. "It's a little surprise, Skipper."

"You know how much I hate surprises, Mr. Dunn."

"I think you'll like this one."

With no explanation forthcoming, Travis turned back to his phone and texted Cal again. None of his previous attempts had gone through. *Must be the weather out there.*

The flight didn't take long, and Travis peered out the window as they neared the airport. Instead of heading to the helicopter pad Travis was accustomed to, the pilot veered the aircraft to the south. He turned to Dunn.

"You want to tell me where the hell we're going NOW?"

Dunn could see he'd maxed out his boss's patience. "We're getting a lift from the 118th Air Wing."

"The Air National Guard?" Travis couldn't remember ever having any interaction with the unit. Their base sat right next to Nashville's airport.

"Yeah. I've got a buddy I served with in the Army. He left the Army and re-enlisted as a First Sergeant in the Air National Guard. I gave him a call and asked if they were looking to run any practice drops. He said yes and the deal was done."

"Did you say practice drop?"

"Oh, yeah. Didn't I mention that we're gonna parachute in?" Dunn's smile reminded Travis of a certain overly-chipper instructor he'd had at BUDS. The damn guy always seemed so cheery about making the SEAL candidates do anything dangerous.

"You've got to be shitting me, Todd."

"Now why would I do that, Skipper?" Dunn asked innocently, the bright smile still plastered on his normally serious face.

———

To expedite the process, the helicopters landed just yards from the waiting C-130 Hercules. Dunn's friend made the quick introductions and had a crew waiting to help load gear.

"You sure this is just gonna be a one way trip, Todd?" the grizzled First Sergeant asked.

"That's all we need. Thanks again for the last minute lift."

"Don't thank me yet. Your pilot, Captain Jeffries, is known as a little bit of a cowboy around here. In fact, his call sign is Cowboy. Might make for a fun ride." He patted Todd on the back and moved to help his men finish loading the packs.

Dunn looked at his friend in confusion then stepped in line to board the aircraft. By the time he got onboard, Travis was chatting with the pilot. Capt. Jeffries looked to be about sixteen years old. Despite his youthful appearance, he sported a very blond and very waxed handlebar mustache. A pair of aviator sunglasses was perched on his head, and he leaned his small frame casually against the plane's bulkhead.

Travis turned as Dunn approached. "Todd Dunn, meet Captain Jeffries."

Jeffries smiled and shook Dunn's hand firmly. "Call me Cowboy." He pointed to the patch on his flight suit that sported his moniker.

"Good to meet you, sir," Dunn offered carefully. He never knew how to handle these non-military-looking pilots. "Thanks for giving us a ride."

"Not a problem, buddy. Thanks to you guys I won't have to fly a thousand circles over Nashville today. Gets boring after the first two turns. Besides, I've always wanted to fly into a snowstorm. Should be fun!" Jeffries really did look like a kid on Christmas day when he smiled.

Travis was enjoying Dunn's unease. He decided to push it a little farther. "Hey, Cowboy, I know Mr. Dunn was just dying to ask you about your mustache."

Cowboy beamed and carefully stroked both ends of the impressive formation. "I know it's not really within military regs, but my boss lets me keep it because of all the trips I take to Afghanistan. It wouldn't be right if I crashed and got captured with my baby face. At least this way the terrorist that gets his hands on me might be impressed by my studly 'stache and keep me in the land of the living."

Dunn didn't know how to respond. Travis just chuckled and moved to find a seat. It would be an interesting flight to Wyoming.

EPISODE 3

CHAPTER 29

Visibility had turned to shit. In order to avoid being split up, Cal's team had opted to close the gaps between men. It wasn't the best tactical decision based on proper troop dispersion, but it was a practical call made out of necessity.

They'd just entered another gully that had only recently been a stream full of running water when an explosion knocked Cal from his feet. As he settled in the snow, he looked around. He could see a couple of the men struggling to get up and find cover. One man had a hand pressed to his bloody face. *Where the hell did that explosion come from?* Cal thought as he crawled over to a rock outcropping and made himself as small as possible. A minute later Gaucho was next to him, his white trouser leg covered in blood.

"You okay?" Cal asked, concerned.

"No problem, boss. Just a scratch."

Gaucho had already applied a hasty bandage to the shrapnel wound.

"Have any idea where that came from?" Cal said as he tried in vain to see anything through the incessant snowfall.

"I'm pretty fucking sure nobody shot at us. I think it was a triggered IED."

"Anybody hurt?"

"Just some minor cuts and bruises. We got lucky because of the snow, I think. I'll bet that damn thing was on a delay or I would've been smoked. We've gotta get off this trail."

Cal nodded. The terrain wouldn't open up for a while. Staying on the narrow trail had been a gamble they'd just been called on. They were sitting ducks despite the snow cover. It would be easy for their enemy to rig traps all along the winding path. Taking to the higher trails would slow their journey considerably, but was necessary considering the alternative.

"Okay. Why don't you run point on the left side of the canyon and I'll take the right. As long as we keep going uphill and don't shoot straight across the ravine, we should be all right."

Gaucho didn't look pleased with the idea of splitting his team further, but he trusted Cal's judgment. The Marine was a formidable warrior in his own right and could handle himself.

"Just promise me one thing, boss."

"What's that?"

"Wait for me to catch up before you take out all the bad guys."

Cal grinned and crawled off to find Daniel.

———————

Trapper peered through his thermal scope. He could only pick up faint blurs because of the blizzard, but he could see that his plan had worked. The small IED wasn't meant to kill anyone, although the ruthless mercenary wouldn't have minded. His goal was to get them to do exactly what they were now doing: separating.

Ponder's second-in-command loved a challenge. Trapper knew that if his boss was with him he would've wanted the attackers killed quickly. "Kill those fuckers right now," he would've said. That wasn't Trapper's style. He liked to take out enemies slowly and methodically.

Trapper loved the hunt almost as much as the final kill.

Cal found Daniel and Lance behind a pile of fallen trees. The men were deep in conversation.

"What's going on, Daniel?" Cal asked over the howling wind.

"Lance thinks the explosion was from his friend Trapper."

"The guy that got away?"

Briggs nodded. "He's some kind of tracker. Lance says he's really good. Tell him, Lance."

Lance looked at Cal uncertainly. "Yeah. Trapper likes the hunt. I think he was an MP in the Army. He gets off on seeing other people in pain."

Cal didn't know what to believe. While he trusted Daniel's judgment regarding their prisoner, he couldn't bring himself to believe in Trapper's former partner. "So where do you think he is?"

Lance pointed up to the ridgeline. "Up there somewhere. He used to bring me over here to scope out the area and check on his hides. He liked to shadow hikers. Trapper said it kept his skills sharp."

"Did you say he has hides up there?" Cal asked incredulously. "Why didn't you tell us about that before?"

Lance looked to Daniel for support. Daniel answered for him, "I asked him the same thing, Cal. He figured Ponder would probably keep Trapper close to home. They don't have a ton of guys to guard the place. I believe him."

Cal knew it was a moot point. "You think you can show us where the hides are?"

Lance nodded. "It might be a little harder with the snow, but I've been here a few times, and I'm pretty good at land nav. I think I can find them."

"Good. The three of us will go together. Daniel, go find Gaucho and tell him what we're doing. I want to have a little talk with Lance."

Daniel stared at Cal for an extended moment then left to brief Gaucho. Cal knew what Daniel's look meant. *Keep your temper in check, Cal.*

Cal turned back to Lance. "I want to make sure we're on the same page here, Lance."

The blonde giant gazed back in confusion. "What…what do you mean, Mr. Stokes?" Lance had seen how the other men respected the young leader. He looked uncomfortable under the Marine's scrutiny.

Cal's eyes went cold. "I appreciate you helping us this far and not giving us any trouble. But I want to tell you that if you so much as think about betraying us, I will take care of you personally."

Lance's face turned serious. "Mr. Stokes, I know what you're saying, but let me tell you something. You guys have treated me nothing but decent. I mean to repay that favor by helping you find Trapper and Mr. Ponder. I won't let you down, sir."

It wasn't the reply Cal had expected. Up to this point, Lance hadn't said a word to Cal.

"Okay. I'll make you a deal. When we get out of this thing alive, I'll put in a good word for you when you look for a new job."

Lance knew it was more than he deserved. He was grateful for the chance. The disgraced former Marine knew that Ponder wouldn't give him the same chance.

"Thank you, Mr. Stokes." Lance reached out to shake Cal's hand.

Cal grabbed his hand and shook it firmly. "Just one thing. Stop calling me Mr. Stokes. It's Cal."

Five minutes later, Lance was leading the way up the steep slope. He'd told Cal and Daniel that Trapper had as many as twenty observation points in the area, but that of those, only two or three were in the immediate vicinity.

The rest of the team was fanning out in pairs, keeping as much dispersion as possible considering the heavy snowfall. Over Gaucho's objections, Cal had ordered the rest of the men to proceed toward Ponder's hideout. He knew they were running out of time. Daniel and Cal would take care of Trapper.

CHAPTER 30

"Have you heard from Cal? Everybody okay after that IED?" Brian Ramirez asked MSgt Trent as they both stopped for a quick sip of water. The going had gotten a lot tougher since they'd left the trail. They had to resort to taking quick breaks both to recharge a bit and to check in with the other teams that were somewhere out in the invisible terrain. Their small radios were struggling to transmit in the storm.

"Last time I had a signal, they were breaking into smaller groups too. Cal said he and Briggs were gonna find that guy that escaped."

"The guy with the nose?"

Trent nodded as he stuffed a whole Power Bar into his mouth. "Cal says the Upshaw kid might know where he is."

"I don't know if we should be trusting him."

Trent just shrugged. "If Snake Eyes thinks he's cool, that's good enough for me. Besides, if Cal takes out Ponder's number two guy, we'll be doing a lot better than we are now, Doc."

Brian had a hard time agreeing. From the start, the whole operation felt like they were three steps behind. It wasn't anyone's fault, least of all Cal's, but Brian couldn't shake the feeling that they were walking into a trap.

After checking in with the rest of their team, Brian and Trent continued up the mountain.

The first hide they found was empty. Lance told them that normally there was a stash of survival goods hidden in a small depression in the back of each small cave. They didn't see any signs of recent passing.

Cal looked down at his watch. They were losing a lot of time looking for someone that might not even be there. "I think we need to split up. The next two hides aren't too far apart. Maybe we can save some time if I take one and you and Lance take the other."

By the look on his face, Daniel didn't like the idea. "We're already spread thin, Cal. It won't take much longer for all three of us to check the other two hides. We might need all the firepower we can get."

Cal knew the sniper was right, but he'd already made up his mind. "Let's split up and then meet at the next checkpoint. If one of us doesn't show an hour after that, we can go looking for each other."

Daniel knew he couldn't change Cal's mind. They reviewed their maps one last time and went their separate ways. Daniel watched as Cal disappeared into the squall. He could only trust that he would see his friend again soon.

Cal felt alive. Being alone in the wintery wilderness, he suddenly remembered what he loved most about being a Marine. He loved the thrill of coming to a brother's aid, even in the face of almost certain death. Cal didn't want to die, but he wasn't afraid of it. Like many other warriors, he'd always hoped that his life would come to a swift end. He'd seen fellow Marines suffer and fight through horrendous injuries only to succumb in the end. No, Cal preferred a sniper round to the head. Instant. No pain.

He shook the macabre thoughts from his head. It wasn't his time to die. He had to save Neil and get his men out alive.

Ten minutes later, Cal knew he was getting close. He stopped to consult his map and study the terrain. Despite having an ultra-reliable GPS, Cal still liked to fall back on his land navigation skills. As long as he had a map and a compass, Cal could find his way.

Confident that he was exactly where the GPS indicated, Cal moved cautiously toward his objective. He didn't want to approach the hide from the most obvious route. It would take him a few more minutes to traverse up and over the objective, but Cal didn't want to leave anything to chance.

Just as he neared the point where he'd decided to stage his pack, he caught movement out of the corner of his eye. He looked around. There wasn't anything in his field of view. Turning back to his pack, he took off his skis and arranged them in a standing X over his gear so he could find it again after clearing the objective. It wouldn't help one bit if he lost all his equipment.

As he stuffed his last spare magazine into one of his large cargo pockets, he heard what sounded like an animal roar. *What the hell?*

Weapon out, he spun in a quick three-sixty. Nothing. *What the hell was that sound?* His breathing picked up as he tried to scan through the snow. He'd have to get back at MSgt Trent for putting the idea of bears in his head. Almost since they landed, Trent had talked about wanting to see a grizzly bear. He even kidded about the bears being hungrier than usual. "If they're so hungry, I'll bet one of those grizzlies would love to catch them some Mexican meat, Gaucho," Trent had joked.

Maybe my mind's just playing tricks on me, Cal thought.

Cal did one last check of the area and picked up the small day pack that had been clipped to his larger hiking pack. It had some emergency rations and a first aid kit. The smaller pack came in handy. At least he didn't have to lug the larger one around for a few minutes.

Stepping toward the steep drop, Cal looked over. He couldn't see more than ten feet down. *Damn all this snow.* Cal tested his footing and crept along the ledge that would take him to a small game path up ahead. He found the passage and did a quick look around to make sure he wasn't being followed. Looking back the way he came, he squinted. *Holy Shit!* He saw a huge form running toward the ledge. An enormous grizzly bear was charging straight at him.

Without a moment to think, Cal turned and sprinted as fast as he could down the game trail. The angry bear wasn't far behind.

Daniel had already found three claymore mines on their approach. Rather than take the time to disable the booby traps, the expert sniper bypassed them altogether. Trapper was watching his back and using some heavy firepower to do it.

Just like Cal, Daniel and Lance staged their gear as they neared their destination. Briggs grabbed his sniper rifle and handed the smaller H&K submachine gun to Lance.

"You know how to shoot one of these?" Daniel asked.

Lance nodded.

"Good. Hopefully you won't have to use it, but here are two extra mags just in case." Daniel handed the ammunition to Lance. As Lance checked their gear one last time, Daniel pulled out the small radio and tried to reach Cal. All he got was static. He couldn't pick up any of the other teams either. As long as they made their rendezvous, they'd be fine.

Daniel closed his eyes and tapped into his heightened awareness. He said a silent prayer and then motioned to Lance that it was time to leave. They moved off quietly, both wondering if this would be the right place.

Cal's lungs burned as he ran. He could hear the bear getting closer and closer. The path was getting narrower as he moved. He had to be careful not to get too close to the edge.

Ducking under an overhanging tree branch, Cal stopped suddenly. Two inches from his face was a thin wire. Cal traced it to its origin on the rock wall and found a claymore mine carefully concealed behind debris. He'd come within inches of having his head blown off.

The grizzly was closing in despite the size of the path. *Maybe I can use this*, Cal thought. He eased his way under the tripwire. Although he hated to do it, Cal unslung his pack and placed it under the deadly trap. Cal quickly opened the main pouch, took out his small emergency kit and stuffed it in his cargo pocket. Next, he extracted one of the compact bags of cold weather rations and tore it open. He ripped each small food packet open and threw it on the ground. *Maybe that'll give me a couple extra seconds.*

Not waiting to see if his trap would work, Cal turned and moved away from the roars of the angry bear.

———

Daniel was the first one to see the small hide. It was obvious that someone had been there recently. Despite the heavy snowfall, he could see boot prints. The sniper slowly stalked toward his objective, checking for tripwires as he went.

"Move another inch and I'll blow your fucking head off," came a voice above the cave. Daniel halted and looked up. He could just make out a white form sitting on the branch of a large pine tree. Daniel couldn't see the man's face but he knew it was Trapper. "Put your rifle on the ground and put your hands up," Trapper yelled over the howling wind.

Daniel did as ordered. He couldn't believe he'd walked right into the trap. The only consolation was that apparently Trapper hadn't seen Lance yet. As his enemy climbed down from his perch, Daniel hoped Lance would have the sense to stay out of sight.

As luck would have it, Lance had just bent down to examine something on the ground when he heard Trapper's voice. Lance froze as he strained to take in the unfolding scene. He couldn't see his former co-worker, but Lance could just barely observe Daniel putting his weapon on the ground carefully and placing his gloved hands on his head.

Lance flattened himself on the ground and started to crawl toward the hide. He stopped again as another figure walked into view. Trapper had his weapon trained on the Marine sniper. Lance didn't know what to do. He wasn't smart enough to come up with some elaborate play to help his friend. Lance decided it was better to sit back and wait. Maybe an opportunity would present itself.

Daniel breathed a quiet sigh of relief as Trapper kept his submachine gun pointed at him. Obviously the man hadn't seen Lance yet. Daniel prayed for guidance.

"Where's the rest of your team?" Trapper asked.

Daniel stood silently.

"I said, where's the rest of your team?"

Daniel smiled. Trapper responded by adjusting his aim and firing a round into the snow next to Daniel's left foot. The sniper didn't even flinch.

"I can't wait to beat that smile off your face, Marine," Trapper said. "Now move."

Trapper motioned toward what Daniel correctly assumed was the hide that he and Lance had been looking for. Like all the others, the observation point was situated along a small path overlooking the ravine.

Daniel ducked his head and entered the alcove. He saw a radio, extra ammunition and claymores lying on the far side of the depression. There was room for almost twenty men to stand comfortably. Daniel was surprised by the size.

"Turn around," Trapper ordered.

Daniel turned and faced his enemy.

Trapper moved into the hide. "Last chance. Tell me where the rest of your men are."

Daniel didn't see the harm in telling the man 'most' of the truth.

"We split up. Some of them are on the other side of the ravine. The rest are probably a mile behind me."

"Why are you by yourself?"

"I'm a sniper. I'm used to being on my own."

Trapper took a few seconds to respond. He'd thought the blonde Marine would have resisted more.

"What did you do with Lance?"

"He's still tied up at the house," Daniel lied.

Not that Trapper necessarily cared about Lance's well-being, but he had been curious about his former colleague's whereabouts.

"So here's what's going to happen. I've gotta go find the rest of your friends and kill them. Since I can't drag you along, you're going to kneel down right there and I'm gonna put a bullet in your head."

If Daniel was frightened, he didn't show it. He knew that when his time came, he would be prepared to meet The Almighty. But something told him that it wasn't his time to go. It might have had something to do with the flicker of movement he saw behind Trapper. Daniel smiled again and kneeled down on the ground.

———•———

Lance had silently followed Trapper and Daniel. He'd overheard snippets of their conversation. Lance knew he had to save Daniel, but he didn't know how. His mind worked desperately to come up with a plan. His lack of brainpower and the uncertainty he felt toward harming Trapper kept Lance from making a decision. He knew deep down that Trapper would shoot Daniel.

Stepping up to the alcove's entrance, Lance took a quick peek into the space. Daniel was slowly kneeling onto the floor. Lance knew he had to move fast or his new friend would die. Knowing it would slow him down, he placed his weapon against the rock wall. Lance paused to steady himself and then ran into the cave.

———•———

Trapper sensed the movement coming from behind. Moving to his left, he pivoted away from the cave's entrance. He stood in shock for a protracted second as he recognized Lance barreling into the room. His surprise didn't last long as he quickly depressed the trigger and rounds reached out at his target.

———•———

Daniel didn't have time to watch. He extracted the blade strapped to his left wrist. Daniel silently thanked Cal for the welcome gift he'd gotten when he joined SSI. Cal had an identical blade that had been put to good use in the past.

The sniper gracefully hopped to his feet and moved toward Trapper.

——•——

Lance grunted away the shock as he felt the rounds tear into his body. The room seemed to move in slow motion as he kept his focus on the wild-eyed Trapper. It seemed like a never-ending stream of bullets coming his way, violating his muscular body. Lance pressed forward through the pain.

——•——

Trapper knew he'd hit Lance with at least ten rounds, but the man kept coming. It was too late when he finally remembered the other man in the room. Turning back to where Daniel had been, Trapper's eyes went wide. He struggled to swivel his aim as Daniel closed the remaining distance, blade leading.

——•——

His heartbeat barely elevated, Daniel silently slid his blade under Trapper's chin to the hilt and twisted. Trapper dropped his weapon as he moved his hands to stop the blade. While the two men locked eyes, Lance barreled in, knocking all three to the floor in a bloody heap.

CHAPTER 31

The bear had stopped its bellowing. *He must have found the pack*, Cal thought as he inched his way forward. The satisfying boom he was waiting for never came as he sat and listened again. *Maybe it was a dud.*

The Marine hadn't found any other tripwires so far, but he wasn't taking any chances. He had to be careful. The thin path was too easy to booby trap.

Just as he started forward again, he heard a loud explosion followed by a frightening scream from the injured grizzly. Cal didn't like killing innocent animals, but if it came down to a fight, he sure as hell was going to do his damnedest to win, even if it meant killing the bear. Cal closed his eyes, waiting for the grizzly's screams to subside. Instead of stopping, they became angry roars and seemed to be getting closer.

Cal hurried to try to close the remaining distance to the hidden alcove. He glanced back and saw the bear moving effortlessly along the ledge. Cal had no choice but to turn back and defend himself.

His submachine gun felt pathetically small as he looked up at the gigantic bear that had now reared up on its hind legs. Cal fired his 9mm rounds into the grizzly's body. The bullets didn't even seem to slow the bear. With lightning speed, it swatted the weapon out of Cal's hands. The gun fell into the whiteness of the deep ravine.

The bear looked at Cal as if to say, *you have two seconds to run.* Cal took the hint, turned and ran. The grizzly paused for a moment to lick its bloody paw, roared, and then followed. It seemed to recognize that its quarry was cornered. The large male knew every inch of its territory. The path ended soon and Cal would have nowhere to go.

Daniel checked Trapper to make sure the man was dead. The beak-nosed mercenary's eyes stared into nothingness.

Lance was struggling to sit up. As Daniel moved to help him, he saw blood seeping out of the big man's mouth. It didn't look good for his new friend.

"Where are you hit?" Daniel asked in concern.

Lance tried to answer but couldn't speak. He looked down at his torso as Daniel ripped the man's coat open. There were too many entry wounds to count. Trapper had done the job.

Daniel reached into one of his cargo pouches and pulled out a small first aid kit. Knowing the dangers of the battle-field, he'd packed it himself long ago. He extracted a small syringe and looked at Lance.

"This will help with the pain."

Lance looked at Daniel with pleading eyes. He knew he was going to die.

Daniel carefully grasped the larger man's arm and injected the powerful drug. The effects were almost instantaneous. It was a special concoction he'd come across while serving in Afghanistan. The Corpsmen and their Marines called it 'sleep juice.' It was used for the worst cases and only as a last resort. There were some times when you just knew an injured warrior was going to die. Better to let a man die in peace. The drug wasn't officially sanctioned by any of the military branches because of its potency and the obvious ethical issues. After losing his spotter in Afghanistan, Daniel had made himself a promise that he would never let anyone suffer the way Grant had. Better to let a man die in peace.

Lance's features softened as the drug took effect.

"Don't worry, I'll get you out of here," Daniel said softly.

Lance shook his head already knowing what would happen. He would die in the cave. With great effort he grabbed Daniel's arm and spoke through gurgled blood, "I'm...a... Marine."

Daniel nodded solemnly and smiled at the dying man. "You won your honor back, brother. I'll make sure everyone knows you died as a Marine."

Lance's smile filled the room. Daniel would never forget the look of pure joy on the dying man's face.

"Close your eyes, Lance. It won't be long now."

The big man nodded and closed his eyes for the last time.

"God be with you, my friend," Daniel whispered, as Lance exhaled his last breath.

The sniper silently asked God to watch over Lance. Then he stood up, gathered a few items, and left in search of Cal.

———

Cal reached the end of the trail and cursed. He was trapped. As he went to brace himself on the steep rock wall, his hand slipped. Cal barely caught himself before he slammed his head. He hadn't noticed it as he approached, but there was an opening. Looking closer, Cal saw that there was a hole about three feet in diameter. *This must be the hide.*

Hoping that there was something inside he could use, he went head first into the alcove. The space was small. Cal figured that it might be possible to fit two men in the tiny cave. Luckily, there weren't any traps awaiting his arrival. He felt around in the dark for anything he could use as a weapon. His hands finally found a stout stick. Cal picked it up and felt along its length. It was barely two feet long with blunt ends. Cal guessed that someone had probably once used it as a fire poker.

The thought gave him an idea. He reached into one of his pockets and felt the butane lighter he always kept there. His hope somewhat restored by the feel of the lighter, he unzipped the parka and started to tear strips off the bottom of his polypropylene undershirt. Cal wrapped the thin strips around one of the ends of the stick. Just as he went to light the improvised torch, the space went completely dark. The bear had reached the cave's entrance.

———

After retrieving his gear from where he and Lance had staged it, Daniel took off for the rendezvous point. Daniel was glad that Cal wouldn't have to deal with Trapper. Maybe the rest of the insertion would go smoothly.

CHAPTER 32

Daniel made good time getting to the rendezvous point. He'd waited impatiently as the minutes ticked away and still no Cal. Finally, Daniel made the decision to find his friend. It wasn't far, and he figured out a route that would ensure the two Marines wouldn't miss each other.

The sniper staged his gear and put on his skis. He tried to raise Cal on the radio. There was no answer, so Daniel got his bearings and took off in Cal's direction.

Cal had managed to light his makeshift torch and look around the small cave. There wasn't anything else he could use as a weapon. The bear had at first searched the trail thinking that Cal had jumped off the side. It didn't take the grizzly long to figure out that his target was right behind him in the little recess.

Man and beast had traded swings and shouts of anger. The huge animal couldn't fit in the hole and Cal couldn't deliver any damage with his measly torch. *Whoever said bears are afraid of fire was full of shit*, Cal pondered angrily as he took another ineffective swipe at his opponent.

Despite the claymore mine explosion and being riddled by Cal's rounds, the bear didn't seem to be slowing down. Occasionally he would step back and lick his wounds, only to come back at Cal's hideout with renewed vigor. Cal knew it was only a matter of time before a claw came far enough in to deal a deadly blow.

———•———

Daniel heard the bear long before he saw it. He could only hope that Cal was on the delivering end of the wrath in the beast's tone. It sounded like something from the pits of hell.

Following the bear's cries, Daniel made his way along the ridge.

———•———

The bear smelled something in the wind. It paused briefly and cocked its ear, straining against the howling storm to hear anything out of the ordinary. Nothing. The creature stood back on its hind legs and sniffed the air. The smell was gone.

It turned back to the cave and gave in to its primal instinct. The mighty mammal roared deafeningly as it knew it would soon have its prize.

———•———

Daniel had eased himself down onto the narrow path. It wasn't hard to pinpoint the location of the bear from all the noise it was making. Gazing through the white downfall, Daniel finally saw the brute. It alternated sticking each arm into the hole almost like it had found a gigantic bee hive filled with honey.

Daniel knew at once that it was Cal the bear was after. He could even see a flicker of what he assumed was a torch coming from the small entry. Daniel couldn't understand why Cal hadn't just killed the grizzly.

The sniper couldn't get a good shot from his precarious position, so he went with another option. He started yelling.

It took the enraged bear a second to hear him over the blizzard. Even when he did turn around, he couldn't pinpoint Daniel's location. The beast sniffed the air again trying to find what had now claimed his interest twice.

Daniel watched quietly as the bear searched. He yelled again and locked eyes with the mighty animal. It seemed confused as to what it should do. *Go after the new human or stay with the one cornered in the hole?* While it was deciding, Daniel watched in amazement as Cal climbed out of the hole, took the quick steps to the edge of the ravine, jumped into the swirling wind and disappeared below.

The bear turned just in time to see Cal jump. Much as a child quickly loses interest in a toy, the bear forgot about its first prey and set its angry gaze on Daniel. Daniel watched in amazement as the gigantic fiend deftly maneuvered its way along the narrow path. The Marine turned and ran back up the trail. He could only hope that Cal was still alive. Right now he had to deal with the enormous grizzly.

Cal tried to keep his descent as close to the ravine wall as possible. He had no idea how far the fall would be, so he kept trying to grab hold of something. The descent was painful as he hit branch after branch and then twisted his knee slamming into a rock only to be thrown down the wall farther. Cal worried that the drop would never end. As soon as he thought it, the ground greeted him with a painful thud. He lay there for a full minute, listening for the bear that he was almost sure had jumped after him. The animal never came.

Cal rolled over onto his stomach and pushed himself into a sitting position. He tested his limbs, amazed that, despite a few bumps and bruises, nothing appeared to be drastically wrong with him. *I think I just used up another one of my nine lives.*

He got to his feet and steadied himself against a large boulder that he'd just missed coming down on. Cal knew he couldn't climb back up, so the only way to go was through the ravine. *Hopefully Daniel took care of Trapper*, Cal thought as he started walking. *This is gonna be a real pain in the ass without my skis.*

———

Daniel glided along the path until he came to a small section that looked just big enough for him to lie on. He skidded to a stop and moved into a prone position on the snow-covered ledge. It would give him the best stability to fire his rifle if he was lying on the ground. The bear wasn't far behind. Daniel knew he would only have time to fire one shot. With minimal visibility, the window of opportunity was finite. He could only see ten feet down the path.

He settled his breathing and searched for the bear through the rifle site. The mammoth beast broke through the blinding snow not twelve feet from the prostrate Marine. Daniel aimed at the animal's head and fired.

CHAPTER 33

"They should be here by now, Top," Brian commented.

MSgt Trent tried his radio again. They hadn't been able to establish contact with Cal or Daniel for hours. He'd found out from Gaucho that the two men had gone off to find Trapper. The normally optimistic Trent was starting to fear the worst.

"I don't know if there's much else we can do but wait, Doc. I'll bet they just got distracted catching snowflakes or something."

Trent's attempt at humor fell flat against Brian's anxiety. It wasn't like the two Marines to be late for anything. Brian was usually the one catching flack for not showing up fifteen minutes early.

"Anything from Gaucho?" he asked.

"I just talked to him. He and his boys are waiting for us at the next checkpoint. Says they haven't encountered any bad guys."

Brian nodded and looked back down the ravine. "Where are you guys?"

———◆———

Cal was slowly making his way up the ravine. Not wanting to walk on the possibly booby-trapped trail, Cal's travel was further hindered by frequent holes, rocks and bushes hidden beneath the winter snow. If he had his skis, he would have glided right over them. But with only the boots on his feet, the going was slow and painful. He'd aggravated his knee worse than he'd thought in the fall. Each step brought a shooting pain up his right leg.

At least he still had his map and compass in his pocket. For some reason, that thought made him push harder. He knew where he was going. Now all he had to do was get there. Cal strained his way up the mountain, thinking of Neil as he went.

———◆———

The buyers had just arrived at Ponder's compound below the peak of Battleship Mountain. They were escorted in by a cadre of Ponder's most loyal soldiers. He waited impatiently behind his desk, sipping from a large glass of Jack Daniels. He already had a few lines of coke earlier to keep his energy levels up. It had been a long couple of days. Ponder hoped the wait would soon be over.

The head buyer was shown into Ponder's office. He was a man of average height and build. Ponder knew the man was from somewhere in the Middle East as evidenced by his complexion and facial features. He hated dealing with Arabs or Muslims or whatever they called themselves. They were all beggars or thieves in his opinion, but in this case they were his meal ticket.

Nick Ponder extracted himself from his chair and moved to greet the emissary. "Welcome to Wyoming!"

The smaller man bowed slightly and smiled. "Thank you, Mr. Ponder. My name is Benjamin," he said with a slight British accent.

Ponder knew it couldn't possibly be the man's real name, but he didn't care. The two men shook hands and took a seat on opposite sides of the desk. Ponder waved for his guards to leave the room. He waited until the door was closed before speaking.

"Did you bring the money?" Ponder asked, trying not to sound too anxious.

Benjamin raised a black case and set it on the desk. "Cash denominations in Dollars and Euros, along with gold and diamonds, as per your instructions. The balance of the purchase price will be deposited into your overseas accounts once we have confirmed delivery with my superiors."

Ponder nodded and inspected the contents of the briefcase. It was only a small fraction of his fee, but still tantalizing. He fought the urge to drool as he fingered the small bag of diamonds.

"When may we see Mr. Patel?" asked Benjamin.

Ponder looked up from his small horde. "I thought we'd have a little lunch and then head down to see your new pet."

Benjamin smiled amiably. "That is much appreciated, Mr. Ponder, but would it be possible to get our lunch while we administer another test on Mr. Patel?"

Ponder gritted his teeth. "I thought we already got past all this."

Benjamin waived a hand in apology. "It's actually not a test to verify the purchase, Mr. Ponder."

"Then what the hell is it for?" Ponder growled impatiently.

"My superiors merely want to initiate a certain operation prior to our departure. Please be assured that as soon as I see Mr. Patel, your money will be wired to your account."

The comment seemed to calm Ponder. The man known as Benjamin knew the next hour would be the most delicate of his operation. It was important to keep Ponder happy. His superiors had sent Benjamin not only because he was one of his country's deadliest assassins, but because he had the rare dual talents of diplomacy and patience. Benjamin felt just as at home with the Prince of Wales as he did with a common street beggar. Upon laying eyes on Nick Ponder, he knew the man would be easily manipulated by greed.

Benjamin smiled again. "Shall we meet with Mr. Patel?"

Neil was lying down on his cot trying to rest. He'd heard the commotion almost an hour before. His time had come. Neil was scared. Never before had he felt so alone. That wasn't completely true. After the death of his mother and father at the hands of Pakistani terrorists, Neil went into a drug-induced nosedive. It was only through the intervention of Cal and his dad that he had come to terms with the murder of his parents. Neil could still hear Cal Sr.'s words: "*I can't tell you that the pain will ever go away, Neil. What I can tell you is that you'll learn to deal with it and get to living again.*" The man had been a second father to the young college student.

The doorway at the top of the staircase opened with a loud groan. Neil sat up and waited for the footsteps to come down the concrete stairs. Nick Ponder was the first to come to his cell door.

"I've got a visitor for you, Neil," Ponder said with a wicked grin.

A tiny light of hope flared within Neil. Could it be his friends?

A man stepped in front of Ponder and peered into the room. "Hello, Mr. Patel."

Neil's eyes went wide with terror. He knew this man. It felt like all the oxygen was sucked out of the room and replaced with unbearable cold. Benjamin smiled evilly and nodded. He turned back to Ponder. "I am satisfied, Mr. Ponder. Let us finalize our transaction in your office."

Ignoring Neil, they both headed back up the stairs. Neil stayed in his cell. The shock of seeing the man he thought to be dead shook Neil to his core. All hope was lost.

CHAPTER 34

It was getting harder and harder for Cal to put one foot in front of the other. *What I wouldn't give for some food right now.* He'd been dehydrated before and recognized the signs that his body was giving. He needed water soon, but stopping wasn't an option. Occasionally he would scoop up a handful of snow, stick it in his mouth and suck on it. Contrary to what most people think, eating snow can actually dehydrate you. Cal knew the only way to get water out of snow was to melt it. He didn't have time for that. It was already way past the time he should have met up with the rest of the team.

Cal reached down for another scoop of snow and took a bite.

"Didn't your platoon sergeant tell you never to eat yellow snow, Boss?"

Cal whirled around at the sound of the voice. A red flashlight flicked on. Rising up from the snow and darkness was Gaucho. Cal exhaled in relief.

"Please tell me Daniel and Lance made it too."

Gaucho's smile faded. "Snake Eyes is here, but Lance is gone."

"What happened?" Cal asked.

Gaucho didn't have a chance to explain. Daniel walked up and put a hand on Cal's shoulder. "I can't tell you how glad I am to see you, Cal. What the hell possessed you to jump into the canyon?"

Cal looked at his friend in confusion. "How did you know...?" His tired mind struggled to put the pieces together. "You distracted the bear."

"I was about to shoot the damn thing when you jumped. I thought you were dead. We were giving you until 2200 and then heading out."

"What can I say? I guess some of your good luck must be rubbing off on me," Cal smiled. "Wait. What happened to the bear?"

Gaucho stepped closer and answered for Daniel. "Wouldn't you know it, this crazy Gringo shot that fucker at point blank range. One shot one kill, right, Snake Eyes?"

Daniel shrugged at the compliment. "It was dead before it hit the ground...the ground that I was lying on. The grizzly's momentum almost got me. I just barely got out of the way as it came crashing down."

Cal shook his head in amazement. Was there anything the Marine sniper couldn't do?

"What happened to Lance?"

"He died saving me," Daniel answered solemnly.

"How?"

"Trapper was about to shoot me when Lance came running in and distracted him. The poor guy didn't stand a chance and he knew it. Trapper shot point blank. He died in my arms."

Cal recognized the grief in Daniel's voice. It pained him to see the sniper lose yet another of his men.

"And Trapper?"

"I took care of him."

Cal nodded.

"Please tell me one of you has some water," Cal almost pleaded.

Daniel pulled a Nalgene bottle out of his coat and handed it to him. Cal had to remind himself not to drink too fast, but his overwhelming thirst won out. He downed the entire bottle in seconds.

"Where are the rest of the guys?" Cal asked once he was partially satiated.

Gaucho pointed up the hill.

"Let's go see about finishing this fucking hike," Cal suggested.

The three men headed up the hill, each rejuvenated by the sight of the other.

The rest of the team was overjoyed to have Cal back. After hearing the story of Cal's suicidal jump from Daniel, no one had held much hope for his survival.

Under the cover of darkness, the SSI warriors prepped for their final journey around Battleship Mountain. They would stick together for the last leg of the movement.

Brian, MSgt Trent, Gaucho, Daniel and Cal huddled together over a map to finalize the plan.

"We'll stay in a column until we get right here." Cal pointed to the map. "At that point, we'll split up and approach Ponder's compound from here and here."

The men nodded. It wouldn't be easy, but it would maximize their chances of closing in unnoticed.

"Any questions?" Cal asked.

Trent raised his hand. "You get word from Travis?"

"Not yet. This weather is really messing with our comm gear. I can't get a signal with either my cell phone or the satellite phone."

"So we don't even know if Neil's still there," stated Brian evenly. He was all about helping a friend, but his feeling of unease grew as they got closer to their objective.

"What can I say, Doc? It's the last place we know Neil was. Daniel confirmed that with Lance earlier."

Brian wasn't convinced, but said nothing. Cal couldn't ignore the look of doubt on his friend's face.

"If you've got something to say, Doc, spit it out."

There were so many things Brian wanted to say, but he didn't want to dampen the men's spirits. "Just ignore me, guys. Must be the cold messing with my Hispanic roots."

"You got that right, hombre!" Gaucho laughed.

The atmosphere lightened. They made their way back to their gear to get ready to go.

Brian followed Cal. "Hey, Cal?"

"Yeah?"

"I'm sorry about that back there. I just can't shake this… vibe I'm getting."

Cal looked at his friend. "I know how you feel. This whole operation has been one big goat rope from the beginning.

Trust me, if I had something better, we'd do it. But right now we need to push forward and find Neil."

"I know."

The two men stared at each other for a moment. Brian broke the silence. "Just avoid jumping off any more cliffs, Staff Sergeant. I'm a good corpsman, but not THAT good."

They both laughed. "Don't worry. I hope I never have to do that again."

Cal patted his friend on the shoulder and moved off to put on the gear the team had managed to piece together for him. As he strapped on his new skis, Cal tried to ignore the nagging sense of dread that threatened to overtake his resolve. Neil and the rest of the men were counting on him.

Travis stood in the cockpit looking over Cowboy's shoulder. They'd been waiting for the storm to die down for hours.

"We're gonna need to get a refill soon," Cowboy offered conversationally.

"How long will that take?"

Cowboy consulted his navigation system. "I'd say no more than an hour and half. The ground crew is already expecting us."

"You can land in this stuff?" Travis down to the roiling clouds.

"It's all about trusting your instruments."

Travis wasn't so sure. "I'll be right back."

He walked to the troop hold to find Dunn. Dunn looked up from the conversation he was having with one of the team leaders.

"Cowboy says we need to get some fuel soon," said Travis.

"We can't avoid it?"

Travis shook his head. "I think we're already on fumes."

"How long will it take?"

"Cowboy says it'll take no more than an hour and a half."

Dunn looked down at his watch. "That means we probably won't be over the target again until after midnight."

Travis shrugged. "I don't know what else we can do. Any word from home?"

"The weather's still too bad to see anything. I'm sure that even if we had Neil to hack into the spy satellites, they wouldn't be able to get us a clear picture."

Travis did not like waiting. He hated to think what might happen if they couldn't parachute in.

"Let's play it by ear and keep our fingers crossed that the weather clears after we get some fuel. Who knows, we may get lucky."

"I hope you're right, Skipper, because I'd really like to get out of this aircraft."

CHAPTER 35

After some haggling, the final wire transfer was made to Ponder's account.

"Now that you have your money, Mr. Ponder, would it be okay to use Neil in your server room?" Benjamin asked politely.

"Now that I have my money, you can do whatever you want with that little bastard." Ponder downed the remnants of his drink and slammed the glass onto the table with glee. He could almost smell the money he'd just made. Nick Ponder was finally a wealthy man.

"You sure I can't get you a drink, Benjamin?"

"My religion precludes me from drinking alcohol, Mr. Ponder, but thank you for the offer. Now, can you show me to the server room?"

Twenty minutes later, Ponder left Neil with Benjamin and his men in the server room. Neil was sitting at the main computer terminal. Benjamin handed him a piece of paper with handwritten instructions. Neil read over the notes and looked up incredulously.

"Are you kidding me? I won't do this."

"Yes, you will, Mr. Patel." Benjamin extracted a pistol from his trousers and rested the barrel against Neil's cheek. "You now belong to my superiors. These are the first orders you will obey from your new masters."

"I won't do anything for you fucking terrorists!"

Benjamin smiled patiently and nodded to one of his men. The large henchman reached over, grabbed Neil's ear with one hand and pulled out a knife with the other.

"You will do as instructed or my friend here will take your body apart piece by piece. We will only take the parts that won't hinder you in your duties. I would have thought that after losing your foot, you would already understand the gravity of the situation, Mr. Patel."

Neil looked up at the man with absolute hatred. This man had orchestrated the kidnapping and murder of his parents. SSI had later conducted a clandestine operation to find the terrorist cell and eliminate its members. It had supposedly been an overwhelming success. Benjamin was supposed to be dead.

"Ah! I see you are still angered and confused by my appearance." Benjamin replaced his weapon and sat down next to Neil. "You thought I was dead, no?"

Neil nodded.

"As you can see," Benjamin gestured to his body, "I am still alive."

"How?" growled Neil.

Benjamin grinned. "My people are not as stupid or primitive as you believe, Mr. Patel. It is quite common for our leadership to employ doubles to ensure our safety. The man your people killed in retaliation for your parents' death was a perfectly crafted duplicate. I have had to stay concealed until the perfect time. It just so happened that my revenge coincided with the wishes of my superiors. You see, Mr. Patel, you have grown as arrogant as your father."

Neil seethed and tears came to his eyes. "You don't know anything about my father, you murderer!"

"I know much more than you think. Now, shall we get back to your first assignment?"

Neil glared at the man he'd killed over and over again in his dreams.

Thirty minutes later, Neil's task was complete.

"Are you happy now?" Neil asked, dejectedly.

"Quite happy, Mr. Patel. The sooner you come to realize the wisdom of complying with orders the first time, the easier your time will be."

Benjamin motioned to his men. One of them picked up Neil and threw him over his shoulder.

As the blood rushed to his head, Neil masked his gloom by sending his mind to a happier place.

CHAPTER 36

Ponder watched as the foreigner prepped the three snowmobiles Ponder had given them. He'd wondered how they would transport the crippled Patel down the mountain, and had asked Benjamin about it.

"We came prepared, Mr. Ponder."

Benjamin waived one of his troops over. The big man walked over with his oversized pack.

"Show Mr. Ponder how we're taking Mr. Patel down the mountain."

The man nodded and unloaded the contents of the backpack. It turned out that the team of buyers had a collapsible sled. Fully constructed, it looked like an elongated cocoon. The sled would be completely enclosed and could be towed behind one of the snowmobiles.

"Aren't you worried about the kid puking inside that thing?" Ponder asked.

The ride down the mountain would be treacherous. Ponder couldn't imagine making the journey inside the sled.

Benjamin smiled. "Mr. Patel will be given sleeping medication prior to our departure."

Not ten minutes later, all of Benjamin's men had their gear stowed on the idling snowmobiles. Ponder walked over to the cocooned sled as Neil was being laid in. He watched curiously as Benjamin administered the anesthetic from a small syringe.

Ponder stood over Neil as the drug took hold. "Have a nice trip, Neil."

Neil looked up at his previous captor. A look of amusement crossed his face. "Watch your back, Ponder."

Ponder's eyebrows furrowed. "What?"

Neil grinned like a drunk. "Oh, you'll see."

Before he could say another word, Benjamin stepped forward and closed and latched the lid.

"What was he talking about?" Ponder asked.

"I believe it was simply the effects of the medication. You never know what a person will say."

Ponder's bullshit radar was blaring in his head. Benjamin looked to be saying the truth, but his instincts were telling him something different. He finally shook the feeling off by thinking about all the money in his bank account.

The bearded mercenary grinned and patted Benjamin on the back, gruffly.

"No problem, buddy. You guys all set to go?"

Benjamin breathed an imperceptible sigh of relief. He'd thought Ponder wanted to press the point. This phase of his operation would be the trickiest. Once he and his men left Ponder's compound he'd feel much better.

"We will be leaving momentarily, Mr. Ponder."

"Well, you guys know how to contact me if you need anything in the future."

"Thank you very much for your work and hospitality."

The two men shook hands and parted.

Benjamin jumped on the lead snowmobile and the vehicles left the compound.

Ponder waited until the large doors closed and then turned to go back to the main level. Between transferring his newfound fortune and dealing with the remnants of the SSI team, he still had a lot of work to do.

———◆———

Benjamin grinned under his mask as his small convoy made its way off Battleship Mountain. It was always fun dealing with greedy Americans. They were so easy to manipulate.

———◆———

Ponder sat down at his laptop and typed his password. He took another sip of his whiskey as the web browser loaded his bank's homepage. After glancing at a small notebook he'd pulled out of his pocket, Ponder entered his account ID and password. He waited impatiently as the website took him through its various safeguards.

Finally at his dashboard, the large man clicked on his account.

"What the fuck?" he whispered.

The screen showed that his account had a zero balance. Frantically, he refreshed the page. The balance didn't change.

Ponder could feel his blood pressure rising. He wanted to kill someone. Picking up his landline, he dialed his broker's number from memory. The man picked up on the second ring.

"Yeah?"

"It's me," Ponder responded, on the verge of exploding.

"I know who it is, Nick. It's like two in the morning here. What do you need?"

"I need you to get your fucking ass out of bed and find out where my fucking money went!"

There was a commotion on the other end as the broker jumped out of bed, knocking several items off his nightstand in the process.

"What are you talking about, Nick?"

"I told you. My fucking money disappeared!"

Ponder could hear the man clicking away at his own computer.

"Okay, I'm in your account. It says here that the money was wired out less than an hour ago. What am I missing here, Nick?"

"I'm putting you on hold. Don't go anywhere."

Ponder replaced the phone on his desk and ran for the server room. The only thought in his head as he blasted past two stunned guards was, *I'm gonna kill those fucking ragheads!*

He berated himself for not keeping a closer eye on Benjamin. Ponder realized too late that his greed had seriously clouded his judgment.

Logging onto the computer in the server room, he tapped his foot impatiently, waiting for the thing to load.

A new window popped up.

"What the hell?"

Words started appearing in the window as if someone was writing.

Mr. Ponder, We will no longer be needing your services. - Benjamin

Ponder picked up the flat screen monitor and threw it against the wall.

"Motherfucker!"

CHAPTER 37

"Get your asses moving!" Ponder commanded. His men were hurrying to comply with the rushed orders. Some were still scrambling to get their clothes on.

After destroying half of his server room, Ponder had run through his compound rousing the rest of his troops. He'd even radioed all his men posted outside the compound to assemble in the oversized garage they were now prepping in. His only hope of getting his money back was to catch the double-crossing Pakistani.

"Take only what you need. We're not coming back," Ponder ordered.

The mercenaries looked up in confusion. One man had the nerve to question his employer.

"What do you mean we aren't coming back? All my shit's in my room!"

Instead of answering, Ponder stepped up to the man, pulled out his pistol, and shot him in the face. The boom echoed then left the room in silence.

"Anyone else have something smart to say?"

They all looked down at their dead colleague in shock, then went back to the task of preparing the remaining snowmobiles.

Ponder breathed heavily as he held his gun out, ready to fire. Calming somewhat, he knew it hadn't been the smartest thing to thin out his already minimal troop strength. At least his men now knew how serious the situation was.

The Ponder Group's sole owner stomped out of the room, his mind in full crisis mode. He had a few last things to take care before leaving. Nick Ponder was planning on never coming back to his fortress on Battleship Mountain.

———•———

Cal's team had made good time getting around the mountain. They were at their final checkpoint trying to get a look at Ponder's hideout.

"Looks like the weather might be clearing a bit," MSgt Trent observed.

Cal looked up into the darkness with his night vision goggles. He couldn't tell.

"We'll break up into the same groups as last time," said Cal to the group gathered near him. "Remember to keep your eyes out for Ponder's guys. Who knows where he's got them posted."

None of the men commented. They knew their responsibilities and were mentally preparing for the final descent toward the hideout. If the enemy presented itself, their training would take over.

"If there aren't any questions, I'll see you boys on the objective," finished Cal.

They dispersed and Cal caught up to Brian.

"You sure you remember how to fire that thing, Doc?"

Brian looked down at his weapon. "Shouldn't you be worried about making sure you don't get lost again, jarhead?"

The two friends looked at one another. They'd left the tension between them behind. Both warriors knew how dangerous this last part would be. It was entirely possible that they could be walking into a trap.

"Doc, I don't know how to say…"

"I know, Cal. Don't worry. You know I never would have missed this. Every one of us is doing this for Neil. You've done good. Shit, we've been through worse, right? I'll see you down there, okay?"

Cal managed a nod as Brian turned back to his assigned team.

I hope I'm not leading these men to their deaths, Cal thought darkly.

———◆———

Just as his team set out, Daniel silently ordered the formation to halt. Through his night vision goggles, Cal could see each man quickly crouch down. He made his way up to the sniper's position.

"What is it?"

Daniel pointed down the mountain. "I think I just saw a bunch of snowmobiles head that way." Daniel motioned to the northeast.

"Could you see how many?" Cal strained to see what Daniel was talking about. He could just make out headlights moving in the direction Daniel had indicated.

"I'm thinking ten to fifteen vehicles."

"Could you make out any of the drivers?"

"No. Visibility is definitely clearing, but it's not that good. I've got a bad feeling about so many leaving at once, Cal."

Cal didn't know what to think. Where were that many vehicles going? *Is it a decoy?* Cal wasn't sure how many men Ponder had. The whole thing was one big guessing game.

"Let's get down there fast, Daniel."

The sniper nodded and motioned for the rest of the men to get up and move out.

Cal did something at that moment that he rarely did. He said a silent prayer. *God, please tell me that Neil is still down there.* When no response came, Cal got back into his position in the moving formation. Time was working against them.

CHAPTER 38

"We're over the objective, Trav," Cowboy announced over the C-130's loudspeaker.

Travis stood up and walked to the cockpit. Keeping his promise, Cowboy's friends on the ground had made quick work of the refueling. Most were combat vets and highly experienced in getting planes back over the battlefield, posthaste.

"How's the visibility?" Travis asked.

"The snow gods must be on our side this morning. Believe it or not, I think it's clearing up."

"That's a relief."

"Now, I'm not saying it's gonna be like a sunny day on the beach, Trav. Your drop is still gonna be hella dangerous."

"You just worry about getting us over the target. We'll let our GPS guide us in."

Cowboy nodded and downed the rest of his third Red Bull. "You wanna stay up here while I get the video feed up?"

"Yeah."

"Give Lieutenant Granes over there a second, and he'll let you take a look."

Cowboy's co-pilot fiddled with his instruments, then looked up.

"I think we've got some tangos down there, Captain."

Travis moved over for a better look. The co-pilot had the aircraft's thermal imaging running.

"Tell me what you see, Mr. Haden," said Lt. Granes.

It took Travis a second to take the picture in.

"That looks like a convoy of some kind. Wait, up on this mountain?"

Lt. Granes nodded. "I make twelve or thirteen small vehicles, or snowmobiles considering the terrain."

"They look like they're going pretty damn fast," Travis observed. "Are they chasing something?" He asked in alarm.

"Let me see." Lt. Granes panned the camera in the direction of the convoy's movement. Seconds later, he zeroed in on a smaller group of three vehicles. "A hundred bucks says that's what the others are after."

"Shit. I wish I knew who the hell they are."

"Who who is?" Todd Dunn asked from over his shoulder. None of the men in the cockpit had realized he'd walked up behind them.

"We've got two groups of snowmobiles down there. It looks like the larger group is chasing the smaller group," said Travis.

"How large and how small?" Dunn asked.

"Thirteen in the big one and three in the smaller."

"Any thoughts?"

"I hope to hell it's Cal in the larger group."

No one answered as they all digested the situation.

Dunn spoke first. "Captain Jennings, do you think you can find a spot ahead of that first group to drop in?"

Cowboy scrolled through his mapping system before replying. "Yeah, I think this'll be as good a spot as any." He tapped the screen to indicate the new drop zone.

"Skipper, have you tried calling Cal again?" Dunn asked.

"Fuck! I completely forgot." Travis hurried to pull the satellite phone out of his cargo pocket. "I've got a signal."

Travis redialed the Cal's phone. Cal picked up on the third ring.

"Trav?" Cal sounded out of breath.

Travis cut right to the chase. "Cal, are you guys on those snowmobiles?"

"Say again? I can barely hear you. My signal sucks down here."

Travis spoke more slowly. "I said, are you on those snowmobiles?"

"No. We just saw them leave from Ponder's place. Ten to fifteen of them, right?"

"So you saw both groups leave?"

"Both groups?"

"Yeah. It looks like the group of thirteen might be trying to catch up with another three," described Travis.

"No. We only saw the one group. Shit, Trav. You don't think they're taking Neil out do you?"

"I don't know, Cuz."

"Wait, are you looking down via satellite?"

"Uh-uh. We're circling overhead in a C-130."

"No shit?"

"No shit."

"Well that changes the game. We're getting close to Ponder's hideout. Do you have enough guys to handle the vehicles while we check out the compound?"

"I think that can be arranged." Travis looked at Dunn who hurried to the troop space to prep their men. "How are you boys doing?"

"I'm a little dinged up but okay."

"You wanna tell me about it now?"

"No. Let me get off the phone so we can start moving. With any luck, Ponder took a few guys with him. Maybe we'll just have to mop things up and leave the real fun to you guys. Are you jumping in?"

"Yeah."

Cal laughed. "You sure your old ass is still up for it? I've been meaning to talk to you about your expanding waistline."

"Fuck you, Cal," Travis said, not without affection. If anything, Travis Haden was more fit than he had been with the SEAL teams. "You call me when you get done, okay?"

"Yes, Dad. Stokes, out."

Travis looked down at the sat phone. Despite the risk, he realized that he'd really missed the fun of being in the field. He turned back to Cowboy. "I'll head back to get suited up." Travis joined his men, a little more swagger in his step than he'd had for years. *To battle.*

———

Cal was now able to communicate with Trent and Brian's team. They'd made better time and were even now approaching the main entrance to Ponder's stronghold. Cal was close enough, and the weather had cleared so he could just make out their forms slowly maneuvering into position. He watched the breach team approach the large steel doors.

He was able to raise Brian on his satellite phone.

"The breach team is checking out the front door," Brian described.

"Yeah, I'm watching right now. No bad guys on the way in?"

"Nope. You?"

"No bad guys. I think they're headed down the mountain chasing someone else."

"How do you know that?" Brian asked.

"Trav's playing guardian angel in a C-130 overhead."

"Holy shit!"

"Yep."

"Hey, I think I see you guys. Wave to me."

Cal waved to the other group and Brian waved back. Just as Cal went to sign off from the call, Brian's waving form disappeared in an enormous explosion.

The sound and shockwave swept over his team as Cal screamed for his friends.

———

"What the fuck was that?" Lt. Granes asked out loud. He'd been monitoring the progress not only of the two groups of snowmobiles but also of Cal's two teams.

"What?" asked Cowboy.

"I think there was just a huge explosion right where the good guys were going."

"Don't just sit there, Granes. Go get Haden!"

Lt. Granes hurried to find Travis.

Seconds later, Travis, fully outfitted for the jump, rushed awkwardly into the cockpit.

"What's going on?" he asked.

"Granes says there was an explosion on your objective. Did your cousin bring a whole lot of C4 with him?"

"No. Let me try to get him on the line. How long until we drop?"

"Under two minutes."

"Okay."

Travis dialed Cal's number. There was no answer. He tried again. Nothing.

"Shit. I can't get him."

"Maybe it's just the weather again," Cowboy offered.

"I hope so."

Travis knew there wasn't anything he could do about Cal's team. He had to focus on stopping the snowmobiles.

Glancing at his wristwatch, Ponder smiled. One of the precautions he'd taken while building his compound was to rig it with enough explosives to knock down a skyscraper. He'd learned the trick from a drug kingpin in Mexico City. The man had described how each one of his safe houses, warehouses and labs was rigged for complete destruction. When the drug lord told Ponder how much it cost, he was pleasantly surprised and filed it away until his own construction began. He'd done the explosives installation himself with the help of some tips he found online on various demolition how-to sites. The cost was minimal and it gave Ponder an added layer of security should his enemies or the authorities show up.

It'd been an easy choice to set the timer. His cover was blown either way. Nick Ponder would never be coming back to Battleship Mountain. The small pack strapped to his back contained the currency and valuables that Benjamin had given him earlier. It would be enough to help him should the need arise. Ponder grinned again, hoping that some of his enemies had been consumed in the blast. The sadistic mercenary only wished he could've watched.

———

At least four of his men were dead including Brian Ramirez. MSgt Trent was badly wounded and unconscious. Gaucho was doing his best to stem the Marine's blood flow. More men were strewn about tending to their wounds.

Cal shook his head in denial as he searched the rubble. The explosion had effectively halved his force and collapsed the entire complex. There was nothing to find. The only reason they'd found anyone was that the blast had blown them all away from the entrance.

———

Travis was shuffling to the open rear end of the C-130 when his phone buzzed. He looked down and saw that Cal was calling. *Shit.* He knew Cal would have to wait. Travis's force had its own mission.

He lowered his night vision goggles and jumped into the darkness.

———

Benjamin had timed the extraction perfectly. On their journey up, his men had staged additional gear as a precaution. They'd just reached the weapons cache and were taking ambush positions. Their kill zone set, Benjamin waited for Ponder to fall into his trap.

Todd Dunn had been the first man out of the aircraft. He and his troops were now floating down through the early morning darkness.

The plan was to land in front of the smaller group of snowmobiles and set up a hasty ambush. Travis hoped that a couple well-placed shots could disable the lead vehicle long enough for them to find out who they were dealing with.

He gazed down through the blackness with his NVGs. *It looks like they've stopped,* Dunn noted. *At least that'll make our timing easier.*

The rest of the SSI operators were cuing off of his descent. It would've been harder to ensure a smooth insertion with moving hostiles. This way they might have a little more time to stage themselves on the ground.

Thank God the damn weather died down, Dunn thought. *The last thing we need is casualties before we fight.*

He watched as the scene unfolded below. It looked like the group was getting off of their vehicles. *What the hell?*

Turning back to the business of insertion, Dunn checked his GPS one last time and prepped for landing.

They'd just rounded a bend when Ponder saw the telltale flash of incoming projectiles. He barely had time to swerve left before a small rocket crashed into the snowmobile next to him. Ponder struggled to stay on his own vehicle but was finally thrown off when he slammed into a large boulder. His body somehow flew over the rock instead of hitting it. The last thing he heard before he slammed into the creek bed was the repeated explosions of more rockets annihilating his forces.

Benjamin smiled grimly as his assassins sent round after round from their shoulder-fired weapons. They'd been a last minute purchase from a Russian arms dealer before leaving Pakistan. Rather than having to rely on accurate aim, the smaller projectiles were, in fact, mini-missiles with heat-seeking capability. The Russian had said that even his dead grandmother could've pulled the trigger and demolished an enemy target. He had not exaggerated. Benjamin made a mental note to thank the Russian and put in a larger order for their next operation.

He signaled for his men to stop firing. Cradling his AK-47, Benjamin approached the wreckage. After quickly dispatching the few wounded survivors, he turned back and ordered his men to get back on their vehicles.

Benjamin took one last look at the carnage and smiled. *Stupid Americans.*

Ponder peeked out from his hiding spot. He winced from the pain of his dislocated shoulder. There were no tears shed as Ponder watched Benjamin kill his men, only seething anger. *I don't care how or when, but I'm gonna kill that fucker.*

He slunk back further and waited for his enemy to leave.

CHAPTER 39

Cowboy had readily agreed to stay on-station for as long as he could. His ability to view the battlefield from the air gave the SSI warriors a distinct advantage. He keyed up Travis to give him the latest intel.

"What have you got?" Travis asked.

"Looks like the smaller group just took out the bigger group. Granes said one of the fuckers actually walked around cleaning up the survivors of the ambush. I think we can safely assume that they're bad guys too."

Travis grunted. At least there would be less of an enemy to confront.

"Are they on their way?"

"Yeah. They're heading straight for you."

"Roger, out."

Cowboy shook his head. The last thing he'd expected to see on his training tour was a full-out battle on American soil. *I might have to stick around these SSI boys*, mused the mustachioed pilot.

———

The snowmobiles were just coming into view.

"Take out the lead vehicle," Travis whispered to the sniper lying next to him.

The expert killer took one last breath and pulled the trigger of his Barrett M107.50 Caliber rifle. Travelling at over 2,800 feet per second, the bullet pierced the lead vehicle's engine and the vehicle sputtered to a stop. A second later, the small convoy stopped right where Travis had wanted. The SSI operators quickly surrounded the three vehicles.

"Drop your weapons!" Dunn commanded.

None of the masked riders complied.

"I said drop your weapons!"

Without warning, one of the snowmobiles gunned its engine and sped off around the others. Travis noted that it was the only one towing some sort of elongated sled. As if on cue, the rest of the riders moved to fire their weapons at Travis's men. The SSI team didn't hesitate. Before the Pakistanis could fire, each man already had an excess of twenty rounds in them.

Travis turned to the sniper who'd stayed next to him in the fray.

"You think you can take out that snowmobile that took off?" asked Travis

"I'll try."

Through his Leupold scope, the sniper tried to find his target in the darkness. In daylight or properly set up, it might've been an easy shot. With darkness limiting his scope's night vision enhanced range, he would be much less accurate. To make matters worse, whoever was driving the thing knew how to maneuver to avoid being shot.

Travis's sniper exhaled and pulled the trigger.

"Hit," he announced, continuing to look through his scope. Despite being hit, the vehicle was still moving. Just as he lined up for another shot, the enemy disappeared into the night.

"What happened?" asked Travis.

"I hit the damn thing, sir, but it's still moving."

"It's okay, O'Brian. We'll have the C-130 keep tabs on it."

Travis went to key his headset when the sniper added, "I think I detached that sled it was pulling, sir."

Travis looked up. "Let's go take a look."

He turned to find that Dunn was approaching. "O'Brian said he might've knocked that sled thing off. You wanna come take a look with me?"

"Sure."

"Can we borrow that last snowmobile?"

"Negative, Skipper. I just checked and it's dead. We must've hit it when we took the bad guys out."

"Then I guess we're huffin' it. Let's grab a couple guys and go."

Dunn nodded and went to fetch some men.

I wonder where the hell Neil is, thought Travis, as he waited.

⬤

Benjamin cursed his luck as he pushed the crippled snowmobile to its limit. Not only had he and his men been ambushed themselves, somehow whoever had attacked them had man-aged to shoot the hitch connecting the vehicle to the sled holding his masters' prize.

There was nothing he could do now. Benjamin put his head down and continued his reckless retreat down the mountain.

They approached the long sled with weapons drawn.

"What do you think's in there?" asked Dunn.

Travis shrugged and stepped up beside it. He examined the exterior and noted that there looked to be some kind of tank strapped to its side. *Oxygen?* he wondered.

Once he determined that the contraption wasn't booby trapped, he unhooked the metal latches holding the medal lid. A hiss escaped as the seal cracked open and warm air whooshed out into the winter cold. Travis carefully lifted the lid and peered in.

"Holy shit! It's Neil!"

CHAPTER 40

Cowboy reported that the only remaining snowmobile had disappeared. With the still unconscious Neil in their possession, Travis had turned his mind back to Cal's team. He'd established variable communication with his cousin and received the news of the team's casualties. Before the connection broke off, Dunn had their men fully ready to head up to Battleship Mountain. They would take turns pulling Neil's sled with a hastily made set of double harnesses. No one complained as they marched through the deep snow.

Upon arriving at Cal's location, Travis took in the devastation. The destruction of Ponder's hideaway was complete.

"How's Trent?"

"He'll live," answered Cal.

Travis could see that his cousin was taking the loss of life hard. He knew the feeling. The former SEAL had lost a lot of friends since 9-11.

"They all knew the danger, Cal." Travis tried to put a comforting hand on his cousin's shoulder, but Cal shrugged it off.

"Did you find Ponder?" asked Cal.

"No. We did a quick search of both groups but he wasn't among the dead."

"So he got away," Cal murmured to the mountain.

"Looks like it."

"Good."

"What are you talking about?" asked Travis.

"That means I can find him…and kill him."

CHAPTER 41

Nick Ponder stumbled into his shabby hotel suite, a Chinese hooker under one arm and a half a case of beer under the other. The suite was surprisingly spacious for the price and the location. He closed the door and shoved the beer into the hooker's hands.

"Why don't you go throw those in the cooler I've got in the bedroom. I'm gonna go take a leak, and I'll meet you in there in a minute."

"Any'ting you wan, big man," answered the prostitute in heavily accented English.

He patted her on the rear, then headed for the bathroom. After relieving himself and rinsing off in the shower, he padded toward the bedroom with a towel wrapped around his waist.

Ponder stopped at the doorway. The light was off. He smiled lustily. *Nothing against Chinks, but I'd rather have the lights off anyway*, he thought.

"You in there, honey?" Ponder asked almost sweetly. It had been a while since he'd gotten laid and his member was already rising to the challenge. There was no answer from the bedroom. Maybe this one liked to play games.

He fumbled for the light switch so he wouldn't trip over the mess he'd left in the room. Through his drunken haze, he remembered that the only light in the room came from a lamp on the bedside table.

"Shit," mumbled Ponder, as he tripped over one of his canvas bags on his way to find the lamp. *Sure would've been easier if she'd left it on, dammit.*

Just as he reached under the lamp shade something came crashing down on the back of his head.

Ponder's head was pounding. He struggled to open his eyes through the searing pain. *What the fuck happened?* A moment later, he realized he couldn't move his arms or legs. Panicking, he forced his eyes open. It took a second for his vision to focus.

He was lying on his back looking up at the ceiling. Ponder looked left and right and saw that someone had strapped him to the bed.

Someone dressed in traditional Pakistani robes walked into view. The person's face was covered with material from a black headdress.

"Who the fuck are you?" Ponder croaked.

The robed figure unwrapped the headdress and stared down at him. Ponder looked back in complete shock.

"You were expecting someone else?" Cal asked.

Ponder couldn't find the words to speak. He'd used every ounce of his skill to cover his tracks.

"I'll bet you're wondering how I found you." Cal smiled and turned toward the living room. "Why don't you come in here, Neil?"

Neil Patel walked gingerly on a new prosthetic device. Assisting him was the blond-haired sniper, Daniel Briggs. Nick Ponder's mind screamed. He was in Pakistan tracking down that damn Benjamin. He'd hoped to somehow kill the Pakistani and re-kidnap Patel. It looked like the double-crossing raghead had lost his prisoner too.

"Double surprise, Nick. I'll bet you thought your buyers had Neil hard at work by now," said Cal.

"How?" Ponder managed to ask.

Now it was Neil's turn to grin. "While you had me shutting down that power plant, I planted a program on your server. It not only infected and tracked that computer, but it also sent all the information about everything you hold electronically back to our servers in Tennessee. The minute I had access to my laptop we started tracking you. We've been reading every email you've sent and listening to every phone call you've made."

"Not too bad, huh?" Cal asked. "We figured you might be coming to get your money back from the Pakistanis. It would've been easy to take you at any time, but 'ol Snake Eyes over there," Cal nodded toward Daniel, "thought we should wait and see how your investigation progressed."

When Ponder didn't respond, Cal continued. "Nick, now you're gonna tell us what you found out at your whorehouse meeting."

Ponder felt like a fool. Already disgraced and dead broke, tomorrow was supposed to be his chance for payback. Not even a week before, he'd been so sure of himself. He was supposed to be on some exotic beach drinking all day and screwing all night. Now he didn't know what to say. Ponder shook the helpless feeling away. His confidence returned when he remembered that he was dealing with Goody-Two-Shoes-Stokes' son. They might rough him up a bit, but he'd been through worse.

"You can go fuck yourself, jarhead." Ponder grinned at his comment.

Cal shook his head. "Go get Higgins."

Daniel left the room to make the call to the battered van on the street below. Two minutes later, Dr. Higgins walked into the bedroom with a leather medical bag.

—•—

As with the FBI agent and the traitor, Ponder talked soon after the drugs took hold. Cal now had Benjamin's location. He'd instructed Higgins to administer the reversal drug that would bring Ponder back to normal awareness. Dr. Higgins nodded to Cal when he felt Ponder was back to his old self.

"Thanks for your help, Doc."

"Anytime, Calvin. I'll be in the van."

Higgins left, surrounded by four robed SSI security staff.

Cal turned back to his prisoner. "Well, Nick, now that we have what we need, we don't need you anymore."

"What are you gonna do, kill me?" Ponder laughed.

Cal stared back, unblinking. Instead of responding, he pulled out a pistol with a suppressor screwed onto the barrel and stepped up to the bed.

"Come on, man. I'm sure we can work something out," Ponder offered.

"We have Neil, the money, and the buyer's location. Tell me what you might possibly have to offer, Nick."

The comment shook Ponder's bravado.

"You have the money?" he asked.

"Oh, didn't we mention that? Because Benjamin had Neil use your computer, we easily tracked the money and took it. So you see, Nick, we don't need you anymore."

Ponder's eyes went wide, his mind finally comprehending the danger. He'd underestimated the Marine's ruthlessness. Before he could respond, Cal extended the pistol and fired two rounds into Nick Ponder's face.

"That was for Brian."

CHAPTER 42

Benjamin relished his early morning rowing on the nearly empty lake. Rowing was a passion he'd picked up while studying at Oxford University nearly twenty years prior. He didn't like much about the Brits, but he appreciated their love of history and sports like cricket and rowing.

After being on the lake for close to an hour, he had worked up a good sweat. In a country where physical fitness was uncommon, Benjamin was a rarity. He never overindulged and, unlike the majority of his countrymen, Benjamin never smoked. His lithe body was a testament to his dedication. There was always the occasional newcomer that would laugh about his workout routine, but that reaction was always their last. The jokester quickly learned that Benjamin's physique was the least of his worries. There was a reason he'd become one of Pakistan's leading terrorists.

This morning's row was especially important because it gave him time to think. His current predicament was aggravating, but did little to unnerve the unflappable assassin. Not only had he lost his entire team, he'd also lost Neil Patel. The only satisfaction he'd received after the berating from his masters was finding out that someone had apparently stolen all the money the Pakistanis had stolen back from Ponder. Luckily, Benjamin had nothing to do with the technological aspect of the operation. Some poor Pakistani geek was probably already dead for failing to protect their masters' funds.

A plan was starting to form in his head as he pulled his racing shell up to the small dock. Standing up, one of his bodyguards handed Benjamin a towel.

"Any phone calls?" asked Benjamin.

"No, sir."

"Good. Pull the car around. I want to go home."

His three bodyguards trotted off down the road while Benjamin finished drying himself with the towel. Throwing on an Adidas windbreaker to ward off the chill, he stretched as he waited, still mulling over his options. The master terrorist still didn't know who had stolen the funds and where Neil Patel had ended up. It bothered Benjamin that a new enemy had somehow ambushed him and probably ended up with Patel. None of the feelers he'd put out had yet to find any of the information he needed.

Benjamin finished his stretches and wondered what was taking his men so long. They'd parked just up the road. He decided to walk down the road and meet them on the way.

After a minute of walking, the car still hadn't come his way. Benjamin cursed himself for not having a weapon. He was getting too lax in his supposedly safe surroundings. Coming around a bend, he spotted the armored black Audi

A8 parked on the side of the road. He could hear the smooth engine purring. *What are those fools doing?*

Because the vehicle had blacked out windows, Benjamin couldn't see inside. Moving cautiously around the vehicle, he made his way to the passenger side. *I'll kill these idiots if they're looking at porn again.*

He'd been forced to find new bodyguards after losing his most loyal men days before. Reaching out a hand, Benjamin went to open the rear passenger-side door.

"Hello, Benjamin," said a voice in English.

The Pakistani whipped around, dropping into a protective crouch as he spun. Standing with his hands casually pointing a rifle at him was a man with brown hair and a sly grin. He'd apparently materialized from the tree line next to the road.

"Who are you?" Benjamin asked.

"I'm surprised you don't know, Benjamin."

He stared at the man dubiously.

"I assure you that I have no idea. It seems that you have the upper hand."

The man nodded. "That's true."

"If you know who I am, I can also assume that you know I am a man not to be trifled with. My men will be here any second."

The stranger laughed as if he were the only one privy to a secret joke.

"I'm afraid your men won't be coming to your rescue, Benjamin."

Benjamin's eyes narrowed.

"Go ahead and take a look in the car."

"Are they dead?"

The man shrugged. A chill ran down Benjamin's spine. *How did he get to my men?* This was his territory. He owned every roadblock and soldier in the area.

It would be unfair to say that the terrorist was afraid. He'd been in too many battles to be frightened by death. It would be accurate to say that Benjamin was concerned. No one had ever gotten this close to him in nearly twenty years. He still bore the scars from the interrogation he'd received at the hands of the Pakistani Intelligence Service.

"How did you do it?" asked Benjamin, now casually leaning back again the sedan.

"It turns out the big wigs in your capital don't like you much. Sounds like you've been a thorn in their side for years. They were more than happy to give us safe passage. That, plus a little cash went a long way."

"So you're here to kill me."

"Not me."

"Who then?"

The young man motioned to the tree line behind him. Benjamin looked and saw a figure emerge. His eyes went wide as the second man limped out.

"Surprised to see me, Benjamin?" asked Neil, as he stepped up next to Cal. He stood with obvious discomfort on a new prosthetic. Neil held a pistol in his right hand.

Benjamin shook his head in disbelief. He could not believe that his countrymen would sell him out to the Americans. After all he'd done for them.

"I supposed there is no way out of this," he asked.

Neil took a second to respond. "I can think of one way."

Benjamin couldn't hide his surprise. "And what would that be?"

"Apologize for my parents," growled Neil, tears coming to his eyes as he spoke.

Would it really be that easy? *These Americans are all alike. Weak*, thought Benjamin.

"Very well," Benjamin shrugged. "I apolo…"

Before he could finish the word, Neil raised the suppressed weapon and pulled the trigger twice. The rounds blasted into Benjamin's chest. He slid down the side of the car and ended up on his ass, clutching his wounds.

Neil limped over to the dying terrorist, his pistol never leaving its target. Benjamin looked up at his enemy in pain.

"Apology not accepted," said Neil.

Before Benjamin could utter another word, Neil fired a single round into his head.

CHAPTER 43

Cal, Neil, Daniel, Travis, Trent, Gaucho and Dunn sat in the weathered leather chairs of the VIP lounge. Each man held a full glass of Tennessee whiskey. They'd just returned from a whirlwind of funerals for their men killed in Wyoming, including Lance. It had been a sobering journey for each of the assembled seven.

MSgt Trent raised his good arm, the other still in a sling, and called a toast. "To the brave men who have gone before us."

Every man raised a glass in silent salute and took a heavy pull from their whiskey.

Cal stared into his glass, thinking about his lost friend Brian Ramirez. He couldn't get the picture of Brian's weeping parents out of his head. They'd hugged him like he was family when, in fact, he'd never met them before.

"Brian told us how much he loved his new friends. He spoke of you often, Cal, and considered you a brother,"

Mrs. Ramirez had said between sobs. He'd held her and wept, the pain finally pouring out over the loss of his friend.

They'd exacted revenge on Ponder and the Pakistani terrorists. There was no one left to kill. It was the inner demons that would take time to fade. Like every man in the room, Cal had lost friends before. He knew there was a grieving process. Cal felt that it got harder with age. Maybe it was a finer sense of one's own mortality and an understanding of the fragility of life.

The bartender, a crusty old Marine Sergeant Major, woke Cal from his reverie.

"Can I get you boys another?"

Everyone looked to Cal for a cue. For some reason he couldn't explain that despite the deadly rescue in Wyoming, every man in the room, including Travis and Dunn, now looked to Cal as their commander. It felt strange, but his years in the Marine Corps had showed him that even the lowliest Marine could be elevated in status through his actions on the battlefield. Unbeknownst to him, Cal's swift tracking and killing of Ponder and Benjamin had cemented him as their leader. In their eyes, Cal was his father's son.

"I think I'll finish this and take one for the road, Sergeant Major," answered Cal. The others nodded in agreement and quietly went back to finishing their drinks. They would talk later.

After receiving their refills, the men said their goodbyes and left to get some much-needed rest. Travis followed Cal to the elevators.

"Can I do anything for you, Cal?"

"I'm okay. I think I'll just get some rack time and then get back to work tomorrow."

"Why don't you take a few days off? There's nothing that can't wait."

Cal shook his head. "I need to stay busy right now, Trav. I'll go stir-crazy if I take time off."

Travis understood. He knew the pain his cousin was feeling.

"Fair enough. Why don't we grab breakfast tomorrow morning and then we'll come up with a game plan."

"Sound good."

Cal stepped into the elevator as Travis paused to answer his cell phone. He motioned for Cal to go up without him.

Cal pressed the button for the second level and waited for the doors to close. Just before they slid shut, Travis's hand stuck in and bumped the doors back open. His face had gone serious.

"What's up?" Cal asked.

Travis extended his cell phone to Cal and said, "It's the President."

Thanks for reading "**Prime Asset**". **If you liked the book, please take a minute and leave a review.** Even the short ones help! Also, please consider sharing this book with your friends via email and social media.

**AS A THANK YOU, GET ANY
C. G. COOPER NOVEL FOR FREE AT
>>> CG-COOPER.COM <<<**

Made in the USA
Columbia, SC
12 July 2019